D1258896

THE
KILLING
LINE

Veteran detective Jack Harris deals with a difficult case
of murder

JOHN DEAN

THE
BOOK
FOLKS

Paperback published by The Book Folks

London, 2020

© John Dean

This book is a work of fiction. Names, characters, businesses, organizations, places and events are either the product of the author's imagination or are used fictitiously. Any resemblance to actual persons, living or dead, events or locales is entirely coincidental.

All rights reserved. No part of this publication may be reproduced, stored in retrieval system, copied in any form or by any means, electronic, mechanical, photocopying, recording or otherwise transmitted without written permission from the publisher.

ISBN 979-8-6153-1816-0

www.thebookfolks.com

The Killing Line is the seventh book by John Dean to feature nature-loving detective Jack Harris. Details about the other books in the series can be found at the end of this one.

Chapter one

When he moves, he's fast. Agile. Lithe. All muscle and sinew. He's effortless when he scales the garden fences, then lands and squats on his haunches and pauses, his head erect, his nostrils quivering as he sniffs the air for the scent of danger. His ears strain for sounds that may indicate that he has been detected. Satisfied that no one is home, his hands move swiftly as he uses a screwdriver to force the lock on the back door and enters the house.

He is into the property in seconds and stands in the kitchen for a few moments, his eyes bright, darting left and right for any sign of movement in the darkened house. When Lee Smedley is sure that he is alone, he moves smoothly from room to room, rifling through the drawers, his tongue flicking with concentration, his long dextrous fingers searching constantly for something of value. Anything of value. Something shiny. Within five minutes, he has gone back into the night, clutching his prize. Three rings left in a dressing table drawer. Not high-end but worth something to the right person. Smedley climbs over the fence again and pauses in the alleyway, body quivering. Then he grins and reveals sharp teeth; he feels excited, powerful, alive.

She, on the other hand, has no life about her as she lies still and silent in the copse less than half a mile away.

Annabelle Roper's hair is spread out on the damp earth to create a golden halo beneath the trees. Pumped full of drugs, the teenager lies with sightless eyes that stare up at the clear, starlit North Pennines night. Her life is done. Taken far too early. Annabelle Roper will never see anything again nor be able to reveal her secrets. And only one person knows she is there.

* * *

The next morning, the atmosphere was febrile outside the Edwardian mansion that housed County Hall. A couple of dozen uniformed police officers were lined up in front of the building, which stood on the outskirts of the town. They had been stationed there to prevent trouble from the growing and boisterous crowd that had gathered. The high-profile presence was designed to counter the tension that had been growing since more than seventy protestors had congregated noisily in the centre of the hillside community of Levton Bridge earlier that morning before setting off in a convoy of vehicles for the hour-long journey down the valley to the county town for their eagerly-anticipated showdown with the councillors.

Made up of people of all ages, the protestors had come to demonstrate against plans to extend the life of a hostel for young boys situated in one of their town's leafy residential streets, and they were determined that their voices would be heard. The mood was ugly as they lined up to lobby the councillors making their way into County Hall for the planning committee which would decide the centre's future.

Filmed by several television camera crews, the protestors chanted slogans and waved banners bearing the words *Close Rowan House* and *We are the ones who need protecting*. Klaxons sounded as the elected members passed through the protestors' ranks, some of them openly engaging with the crowd, smiling reassuring smiles and promising their support, others grim-faced as they ignored the abuse being hurled in their direction. One councillor reacted angrily and shouted something, an action that was greeted by howls of derision and cries of 'shame'. The councillor stuck up a single finger and stalked into the building to a crescendo of catcalls.

Detective Sergeant Matty Gallagher walked over to his boss. Detective Chief Inspector Jack Harris was standing beneath the trees on the edge of the car park, watching the scene unfold in grim silence. Both officers were based in Levton Bridge and had viewed the growing tension in the town with concern over recent days as the date for the council meeting neared.

'The natives would appear to be angry, Kemosabe,' said Gallagher.

'So would you be,' said Harris. 'We had another break-in last night.'

'That's all we need. Where was this one?'

'Nightingale Road. The big white house on the corner.'

'Usual MO?' asked Gallagher.

'Yup. Back door forced, jewellery nicked. The old dear is devastated. One of the rings had been in the family for more than a hundred years.'

'You thinking it's Lee Smedley?'

'I'm always thinking it's Lee Smedley, Matty lad,' said Harris. 'Him or one of his little pals. I asked Alison to bring him in but when she went to Rowan House, they said he had already left for school. And when she checked with Roxham Comp, guess what they told her?'

'That he didn't fancy double geography?'

'Right first time. None of the staff have seen him since yesterday afternoon.'

'Not exactly a surprise,' said the sergeant. 'Our Mr Smedley does not strike me as the academic type.'

Neither detective spoke for a few moments. They were very different men; Jack Harris, born and bred in the valley, was strong-jawed, had thick brown hair without a hint of grey, and was a man of few words. Matty

Gallagher, a decade younger, a Londoner who had moved reluctantly to the area so that his wife could be near her aged parents, was smaller than his boss, stocky, his black hair starting to thin; a man, some said, with the appearance of a monk.

The sergeant spotted a slim fair-haired man in a grey suit, who was in earnest conversation with some of the protestors, his hands gesticulating to emphasise his point.

'I see that our Mr Roper is stirring things up again,' said the sergeant. 'I heard that he was offering them legal advice now. I wonder how much he's charging for that then? Lawyers don't exactly come cheap, do they?'

'He's doing it for free, apparently. I tell you, Matty lad, the man's on a crusade after what happened to his beloved Annabelle. Blames Rowan House for corrupting her.'

'But she denied it,' said Gallagher. 'Said that her vanishing act was entirely voluntary. And she was adamant that no one forced her to smoke the weed. All done in somewhat fruity language when Alistair interviewed her, I seem to recall.'

'It seems that her father has more faith in his daughter's morals than she does.' Harris watched as David Roper gesticulated again. 'He won't stop until Rowan House has been closed down. He'll be in his element today.'

'Certainly looks it.' A loud cry went up from the protestors as another councillor waved angrily in their direction only to be greeted with abuse. 'Jeez, this is turning really nasty.'

The detectives watched as a couple of uniformed officers moved in to talk to some of the protestors, an action that led to a furious exchange.

'They'll get themselves arrested if they're not careful,' said Gallagher. 'I know uniform are under orders not to inflame the situation but I'm not sure they'll have much alternative if this goes on.'

'Yeah, someone is really whipping this up.'

'I had a look at their Facebook page last night. You should see some of the things they're saying about the councillors.'

'Probably deserved it.'

'But this went beyond the norm,' said the sergeant. 'Some lad calling himself Ricky B was particularly inflammatory. He really does not like James Hall at Rowan House. Seems to have a real beef with him.'

'About what?'

'Not sure. It's all pretty obtuse. Just a load of veiled references to him letting the boys down.'

'Do we know who Ricky B is?' asked Harris.

'No, it's just a shadowy picture and I'm pretty sure that it's a fake name anyway. They very often are on Facebook. I guess our techy types could find out easily enough, though. Want me to ask them?'

'Please.'

Harris's attention was caught by a placard at the back of the group. *Remember Ellie*, it said. The inspector frowned. How could he forget young Ellie Cross? She was certainly not far from his thoughts but did Rowan House have a connection with the teenager's death at her Levton Bridge home the previous month after taking MDMA? Police enquiries had ruled out any connection, something Rowan House's outspoken manager James Hall had reiterated whenever the opportunity had arisen. And yet a lingering doubt had remained in the inspector's mind. A sense of something overlooked. Something that he and his team had missed. He believed that the young people of the town knew more than they were letting on. And always there in the inspector's mind was the fear that it might happen again.

Gallagher had spotted the placard as well.

'Thought we ruled out a link with Rowan House,' he said.

'We did.'

'Too much fake news for my liking,' said the sergeant. A particularly loud shout went up from the crowd. 'Someone is definitely playing games. There's several faces I don't recognise.'

'I was thinking the same.'

'You thinking it might be outside influences?'

'Possibly,' said Harris. 'But if it is, I'm not sure I understand why. However, if this Ricky B character *is* behind it, I want to know why he's sticking his neb in.'

'I'll talk to our techies. Anything else of interest come in overnight? I came straight from home, didn't have chance to ring the office.'

'No, all quiet,' said Harris. 'Just as well; we've got enough on our plate with this little lot.'

* * *

Glenis Roper was just about to leave her home in Levton Bridge to go to the supermarket when the phone rang. She hesitated with her hand over the receiver on the hall table, her action stayed by a sixth sense that something was wrong. She picked up the receiver.

'Mrs Roper?' said a young man. He sounded uneasy. 'It's Graham in the office at Roxham Comprehensive School. I am sorry to trouble you but I thought I had better let you know that Annabelle has not arrived at school this morning.'

'She hasn't?' Glenis felt her heart begin to pound.

'I am afraid not, no. We gave it a while in case she had a doctor's appointment or something like that and had maybe forgotten to tell us, but she still has not arrived so we thought we should let you know.' Graham hesitated for a moment. 'Especially after what happened last time. She shouldn't really be missing lessons in a GCSE year.'

'No, of course not,' said Glenis. It was an automatic response that masked the thoughts running through her head.

'Do you know where she might be?'

'I am afraid I don't.' Glenis tried to sound calm but her voice trembled slightly and her palms felt clammy. The receiver shook in her hand. 'She was on a sleepover last night. With Lorna Rudge. Has she turned up for school?'

'She has, yes.'

'I'll ring her mother, see if she can help.'

'That would be useful. I'm sure there's nothing to worry about.' But something in his voice suggested that he did not believe it. Not after what happened last time.

'I'm sure you're right.' Glenis did not sound convinced either.

She ended the call and dialled the number.

'Jane,' she said. 'It's Glenis. I've just had the school on saying that Annabelle did not arrive for classes this morning. She *did* stay with Lorna last night, didn't she?'

'No.' Jane Rudge sounded surprised. 'Was she going to?'

'I thought she said she was.' Glenis tried to sound unconcerned. 'Not to worry, I'll ring round some of the other parents. I'm sure that there's a perfectly innocent explanation.'

But she knew that there wasn't. A mother always knows.

Chapter two

'I don't envy you having to address the meeting with them in this mood,' said Gallagher as the arrival of another councillor outside County Hall prompted more catcalling. 'Whatever you say, it's going to hack someone off. Talking of which, I think that someone wants to talk to you. If you look close enough, you can just about make out her high horse.'

He pointed and Harris sighed.

'That's all I need,' he said.

A middle-aged woman wearing a T-shirt bearing the words *Close Rowan House* had detached herself from the conversation with David Roper and was striding resolutely towards the officers. As Miriam Canley approached, she gave Harris a stern look.

'Whose side are you on, Jack?' she demanded.

'I'm fine, thanks, Miriam. And I don't do sides, I've told you that before. However, we *have* objected to the application.'

'So, you are going to tell the councillors what's been going on then? Our community needs protecting from these young hoodlums.'

'I'll tell them the truth,' said the inspector.

'But whose truth, Jack?'

'*The* truth, Miriam, and it's DCI Harris to you.' A loud cry went up from the crowd as they targeted another councillor who was walking up the path towards the main entrance. 'And might I suggest that your people tone it down a bit?'

'I don't see why we should.'

'We don't want it getting out of hand,' said the inspector. 'If this carries on, some of you are going to spend the rest of the day in a cell and that won't do anyone any good.'

'It would help draw attention to our cause.'

Harris glanced at the television trucks lined up on the far side of the car park.

'I think you've probably done that already,' he said. 'However, some of your people's behaviour is really not acceptable and if you push us too far, we will have no option but to make arrests.'

The parish council chairwoman opened her mouth to reply but something about the resolute expression on the detective's face stopped her. Everyone in Levton Bridge knew that you rarely won an argument with Jack Harris and that he had a long memory when it came to people who crossed him. Noticing that the last of the councillors had entered the building, she gave the detective a final disgusted look, turned and made her way into County Hall, followed by a delegation of protestors. The detectives were the last to enter the building.

'Here goes nothing,' said Harris.

'Politics,' said Gallagher as they walked along the corridor towards Committee Room 3. 'Don't you love it?'

* * *

The call came through to the control room at Levton Bridge Police Station just after 10:30am.

'Hello, police,' said the female operator. 'How can I help you?'

'My name is Glenis Roper,' said a shaky voice.

'Yes, Mrs Roper. How can we help you?'

'My fifteen-year-old daughter has gone missing and I fear that something terrible may have happened to her.'

'Is this Annabelle?'

'Yes, yes, it is.'

'I believe that she did the same thing several weeks ago, did she not?' said the call handler.

'She did, yes.'

'And I seem to recall that she turned up a few hours later, high on drugs.'

'She did, and I'm really worried that she's done it again.'

'I understand your concern, Mrs Roper, but I'm sure that there's nothing to worry about,' said the call handler. 'However, let me take some details anyway. We'll see if we can find her for you, lovey.'

* * *

As the officers approached Committee Room 3, Matty Gallagher produced a sheet of paper from his jacket pocket and passed it to his boss.

'The stats you asked for,' he said. 'They're correct up until yesterday morning so you'll have to factor in last night's job at Nightingale Road if you're sure it's down to Smedley. It's certainly his MO. Don't expect a Christmas card from anyone at Rowan House, will you?'

Harris nodded his thanks, strode to the front and sat down on one of the chairs lined up along the side of the room, not far from the large oval table around which were gathered the elected representatives and a number of council officers. For a few moments, the inspector scanned the statistics that Gallagher had given him then looked up at the protestors who were taking seats in the public area at the back of the room. He glanced at Miriam Canley, looked down at the figures again and pursed his lips; the inspector knew how it would look. Jack Harris disliked giving anyone the impression that he was doing their bidding, but you could not argue with the figures…

Gallagher sat down on the back row. His attention settled on a sallow young man in jeans and a parka, who was sitting two rows in front of him. The sergeant had noticed him arrive outside County Hall during the protest in the company of two other young men who he also did not recognise. Gallagher wondered if he was looking at Ricky B. The young man turned round, noticed the sergeant staring at him, averted his gaze and turned quickly back to face the front.

The noisy buzzing of the protestors' conversations died away as committee chairman Gerald Gault, a grey-haired man in a dark suit that had seen better days, began the meeting. Once the preliminaries had been performed, he looked gravely at the protestors.

'Given the large number of people here, I have decided to take item 7 next,' he said. The chairman gave the protestors a stern look. 'I have consented to your request to allow Mr Roper to speak on your behalf, but may I ask that members of the public act with a sense of decorum? I appreciate that emotions are running high but several councillors have been the victim of angry exchanges in recent days as well as unwarranted comments on social media. Such behaviour does little to serve the cause of democracy, I would suggest.'

There were a few angry mutterings and a man shouted 'Make the right decision, then, you silly old fool.' Both Harris and Gallagher scanned the gathering but could not work out who had spoken. Gerald Gault waited for the noise to die down.

'Item 7,' he continued, 'is an application from the County Council to grant itself approval to turn the temporary planning permission for Rowan House into a permanent one.'

More muttering.

'As I am sure you all know,' said Gault, 'Rowan House is a residential halfway facility to help male teenagers who have found themselves involved with the youth justice system. Although this committee must restrict itself to planning considerations only, the centre manager has asked if he can say a few words. James Hall, please.'

Hall, a slim, thin-faced, smartly dressed man in his mid-thirties, stood up. A low rumble growled its way round the room.

'Thank you, Mister Chairman,' said Hall. 'I felt that you should be in possession of all the facts before you make your decision. There has been a lot said and written about Rowan House in recent months, just about all of it half-truths and, in some cases, downright lies born out of ignorance and devilment.'

More disagreement rippled round the room.

'You can do that all you like,' said Hall, raising his voice to be heard above the hubbub 'but it won't change the importance of the work that Rowan House is doing. And I am not going to let that work be derailed by mob mentality. Yes, some of the young men who stay with...'

His next words were drowned out by shouting from the protestors.

'Please,' said the committee chairman, 'let him be heard.'

An uneasy silence settled on the room.

'Thank you, Mr Chairman,' said Hall. 'All this anger creates a sense of confrontation that is very unhealthy for the Levton Bridge community, I would suggest. I contend that we need to be allowed to continue our work to rehabilitate the troubled young men who stay with us. We are already producing encouraging results.'

'Tell that to the people who have been burgled!' shouted someone.

Loud applause broke out.

'Please,' said the chairman again. He held up his hands. 'Can we debate this like sensible human beings?'

Hall spoke for another couple of minutes and sat down to silence. The chairman looked across to Harris.

'Among the many written notices of objection to this planning application is one from the local constabulary,' he said. 'I felt it important that we should hear more and Detective Chief Inspector Harris has kindly volunteered to offer some thoughts on behalf of the divisional commander, who is unable to attend the meeting due to a prior engagement.'

Gallagher gave a slight smile as his boss stood up. Everyone at Levton Bridge Police Station had heard Harris muttering angrily for days about 'being thrown under the bus' by Philip Curtis, who had blamed a meeting at police headquarters for his non-attendance. 'How convenient,' Harris had said to anyone who would listen. Not that anyone did.

'Chief Inspector Harris,' said Gault. 'Why has the police force objected to this planning application?'

'Because,' said Harris, glancing down at his piece of paper, 'since Rowan House opened just under a year ago, crime in Levton Bridge has gone up eleven percent, following a number of years in which it had been falling. I am not saying that the rise can all be attributed to the residents, but we nevertheless believe that some of the young men are responsible for a significant number of the additional offences.'

'But this is petty crime, is it not?' said Gault.

Harris gave him one of his looks.

'I do not regard any crime as petty,' he said. 'A shed break-in can be as traumatic as a street robbery for some people and there is plenty of research to indicate that fear of crime is greater in rural areas than in towns and cities. A single crime here, however small you may regard it to be, Mr Chairman, can have a devastating effect on the community.'

Applause from the protestors.

'Also,' said Harris, 'there have been a number of incidents involving some of the young men from Rowan House who we believe have been using and supplying cannabis. Such a scenario is clearly a great cause for concern, given the tragic death of Ellie Cross last month.'

A more sombre atmosphere settled on the room and there were murmurs of agreement.

'But,' said Gault after a few moments, 'I understood that Ellie died from taking MDMA, not cannabis?'

'I do not share society's laissez faire attitude to cannabis, Mr Chairman,' said Harris. 'In my view, we have become far too lax. Cannabis is a gateway drug and I can cite plenty of cases in which youngsters started with cannabis then moved onto harder drugs. Turning a blind eye is not a risk that I am prepared to countenance.'

More applause rippled round the room.

'And you feel that closing Rowan House will eradicate the problem, do you?' asked Gault.

There was an edge to his voice and the councillor did not look convinced. Harris was not surprised; Gerald Gault had been a vocal supporter of the project from its early days. Some said that it was his idea and that without his support the project would never have happened, that he had staked his reputation on its success. Gerald Gault was a man with a lot to lose.

'In my view,' continued Harris, 'the county council's experiment would be better suited to a more urban area. Assuming that it is something we should be supporting at all.'

'But do you not have sympathy with the view that Rowan House is helping these young people to reform?' asked Gault. He could not contain his dismay. 'Surely, you acknowledge that this is a ground-breaking project? One that seeks to break the cycle of offending which sees these young people continually finding themselves in trouble with the police? I believe it is known as a "revolving door".'

Gault glanced at James Hall, who was sitting nearby. Hall nodded.

'Rowan House is a project,' continued Gault, his voice rising, the passion clear, 'that seeks to change that situation by giving the boys a second chance. Why, it has even been shortlisted for a national award.'

'I don't do awards,' said Harris curtly. 'As for it being for the good of the community, I would suggest that you talk to some of the people who have been burgled. As a police force, we cannot ignore what has been happening and neither, I would suggest, can this committee.'

The applause was thunderous as he sat down.

'Thank you, Chief Inspector,' said Gault bleakly.

He looked in the direction of the public seating.

'Mr Roper,' he said. 'Did you wish to say anything in response, on behalf of the local residents?'

David Roper nodded and stood up.

'I certainly do,' he said.

The councillors' debate that followed his address grew increasingly heated as one hour dragged on into two, with the members who wished to prolong the experiment pitted against those who wanted to see Rowan House closed, led by representatives from Levton Bridge who were acutely conscious that they were less than eighteen months away from a local election. The discussion was punctuated by frequent interruptions from the gallery and, with the debate threatening to go into a third hour, the chairman looked round the table.

'Ladies and gentlemen,' he said wearily, 'I think that we have discussed this enough. May I ask for a show of hands for those wishing to extend the planning permission for Rowan House?'

Six hands went up.

'And those against?' he asked.

Another six went up.

'The vote is tied,' said Gault. 'As chairman, I have the casting vote. I see much merit in the views so fervently expressed by the protestors but I also have sympathy with the arguments put forward by James Hall on behalf of Rowan House. If we are to truly tackle the revolving door, we have to do things differently.'

The tension was growing in the room as all eyes were turned on the chairman. The protestors held their breath, James Hall seemed fascinated by one of his fingernails and Harris looked gloomy; he could see where this was going and he didn't like losing.

'My vote goes in favour of extending the planning permission,' said the chairman.

The room erupted in uproar and, as the chairman struggled to regain control, Harris looked across at Gallagher then nodded towards the door and the two detectives slipped away.

'No surprise there,' said Harris as they walked briskly along the corridor. 'Gault was always going to back it. He's mentioned in the shortlisting for the national award, after all, and if the council had decided to close Rowan House down, he'd miss out on his chance to meet Prince William, wouldn't he? And blow his chance of an MBE to boot, I dare say.'

'Oh, you're such a cynic,' said Gallagher.

'And don't you forget it, Matty lad.'

The officers had just walked into the car park, ignoring questions from the protestors still gathered outside County Hall, when they were approached by a slim young woman with short blonde hair, wearing a dark suit.

'What's up?' asked Harris as he noticed the grim expression on Detective Constable Alison Butterfield's face.

'Sorry, guv,' she said. 'Tried to ring but you had your phone turned off so the DI suggested I come down and find you. I am afraid that we've got a problem. And it could be a big one.'

Chapter three

'And Annabelle Roper's mum has no idea where she might be?' asked Harris.

'Not a clue,' said Butterfield.

'Sounds like a re-run of last time,' said Gallagher.

The detectives were standing under the trees on the edge of the County Hall car park, talking in low tones to avoid being overheard by any of the protestors who might wander past. They were acutely aware of the incendiary ramifications of Annabelle Roper's second disappearance in a matter of weeks, and the last thing any of them wanted was to be responsible for increasing the tension already thick in the air. It had been bad enough the last time Annabelle vanished, a matter of days before the death of Ellie Cross, with her father angrily demanding police action against Lee Smedley when it emerged that the teenagers had been together.

'And how *is* Mum?' asked Harris.

'Going spare,' replied Butterfield. The detective constable glanced round to ensure that no one could hear. 'She's absolutely convinced that something bad has happened to the kid. Says she's got a feeling.'

'When was Annabelle last seen?' asked Gallagher.

'Late yesterday afternoon. Stayed for netball after school then headed off. She told her mum that she was going to stay overnight at a friend's.'

'Same girl that she was found with the last time?' asked Gallagher. 'Tracey Malham?'

'No, different kid. Lorna Rudge. They're in the same class.'

'Trustworthy?' asked the sergeant.

'Pretty much, I'd say,' replied Butterfield. 'Certainly nothing like Tracey Malham. The Ropers banned Annabelle from knocking around with her after what happened.'

'I'm not surprised,' said Gallagher. 'Bad influence that one. Too much of the *Am I Bovvered?* about her.'

Harris looked quizzically at him.

'You really must get a telly, guv,' said the sergeant. He looked at Butterfield. 'So, the Ropers were happy to let Annabelle stay with Lorna Rudge, were they?'

'I'm not sure that happy is the word. It was the first time that they had let her do anything like that since her vanishing act, but she'd kept badgering them and they knew that Lorna was OK.'

Harris sighed and watched without much enthusiasm as the first protestors started to emerge from County Hall to convey news of their defeat.

'This could get very messy,' he said. 'I take it we checked with Lorna's parents? Not just a simple misunderstanding?'

'I am afraid not,' said Butterfield. 'Lorna's mum did not know anything about a sleepover. Neither did Lorna, for that matter, but the Ropers did not suspect that anything was amiss because Annabelle promised faithfully that she'd be a good little girl and report in during the evening.'

'And did she?' asked Gallagher.

'Three times. Said she and Lorna had done some homework then watched a DVD. The alarm bells only started ringing when she didn't turn up for school this morning.'

'And Tracey Malham?' asked Harris. 'Does she know anything about this?'

'She told her teacher that she doesn't.'

'Mind, we've heard that before, haven't we?' said Gallagher. He looked at the inspector. 'Too many kids round here keeping secrets, for my liking.'

Harris nodded.

'Anyway,' said Butterfield, 'uniform are going to keep an eye out for Annabelle.'

'They could start with Rowan House,' said Gallagher. 'The last time this happened, she and Tracey had been with a couple of their lads. Lee Smedley and Danny Cairns. The girls were found sleeping behind the bandstand, weren't they? Stoned out of their tiny minds.'

'They were, yes, but I put a call in and none of the staff at Rowan House have seen her,' said Butterfield. 'And the school asked Danny Cairns but he knew nothing about it. To all intents and purposes, Annabelle Roper has vanished.'

'As has Lee Smedley,' said Harris. 'I think we can safely surmise that they were together again last night.'

'We worried?' asked Gallagher, looking at his boss. 'I mean, are we thinking that it could be connected to what happened to—'

'Best not to get ahead of ourselves,' said Harris. 'There's nothing to suggest that the kid has come to any harm this time.'

Gallagher nodded.

'You're right, of course,' he said. 'Teenagers go missing all the time. There's probably an innocent explanation.'

'Hopefully,' said Harris. He looked at Butterfield. 'Tell uniform that I want things low key, will you? The last thing we want is a major flap when it could be that the kid is perfectly fine. Folks are aeriated enough without us adding to it.'

The detectives noticed David Roper emerge from County Hall with a group of protestors. They were deep in animated conversation as they walked towards those waiting outside.

'He won't be impressed by what's happened,' said Gallagher. 'He was livid when he heard that Annabelle was telling folks she was Smedley's girlfriend. Somehow, I don't think a scroat like Lee Smedley fits in with David Roper's worldview and if she's with him again…'

He did not complete the sentence, he did not need to.

'Does he know?' asked Harris, glancing at Butterfield.

The constable watched as Roper switched on his mobile phone and immediately took a call. They watched as his expression turned darker and he looked furiously at the detectives.

'I suspect he does now,' she said.

Roper ended the call and strode over to the detectives.

'Did you know about this?' he asked angrily. He jabbed a finger at Harris. 'Did you let me stay in there when you knew that my daughter had—'

'I've only just found out myself,' said the inspector.

'Well, what are you going to do about it? If it turns out that my daughter is with that Smedley kid again—'

'Let's not jump to conclusions, David.'

'Not jump to conclusions!' exclaimed Roper. 'My daughter is missing! What other conclusion is there, Chief Inspector? Well, I hope that you've got people out looking for her.'

'We have, yes, and I am sure that there is absolutely nothing to—'

'Bloody councillors.' Roper snorted and looked towards County Hall. 'I hope they're proud of what they have done. Especially that damned fool of a chairman. Banging on about giving the likes of Lee Smedley a second chance! How many bloody chances does he want? Well, I want the little toerag found and locked up.'

'There's the matter of a little thing called evidence,' said Harris.

'How much bloody evidence do you want?' Roper glared at him. 'There's something not right about that boy and well you know it. He's bloody feral, that one.'

Not giving Harris opportunity to reply, Roper turned on his heel and strode back to re-join the protestors. Within seconds, he was involved in an angry conversation and several of the protestors shot ugly looks at County Hall. Gallagher noticed that the young man in the parka was among them, gesticulating as he emphasised a point.

'So much for keeping things low key,' said Gallagher. 'This will be ideal ammunition for them. If she *is* with Lee Smedley, you can bet your bottom dollar that they'll make good use of the fact.'

'I fear that you are right,' said the inspector. 'Let's just hope that she's not…'

* * *

Shortly before 11:45am, the middle-aged woman and her dog made their way across the playing field behind Rowan House, heading as they always did at this time of the morning for the copse on the far side and the road home that lay beyond it. As they approached the trees, the dog sniffed the air, gave a whimper and ran off at speed. The woman called his name but he ignored her and entered the copse where he disappeared from view and started barking.

'Every time,' she said with a sigh. 'Someone should shoot those bloody rabbits.'

She continued to call the animal but the barking continued with an intensity that she had not heard before. Sensing that something was wrong, she hurried over to the copse where she found the dog crouched over a shape on the ground.

'What are you…' she began but her voice tailed off as she saw what he had found. 'Oh, please God, no.'

She edged over to the trembling dog. Crouching down and clipping the animal onto its lead, she murmured soothing words until it calmed down then forced herself to look closer, hoping against hope that the young girl with the golden hair was alive. After a few moments, it was clear that the hope was a vain one and the woman took her mobile phone out of her coat pocket and dialled 999 with trembling fingers. She requested to be put through to the police, struggling to keep her voice steady.

'Levton Bridge Police,' said the operator. 'How can we help you?'

'I've found a young woman. Behind Rowan House. I think it's Glenis Roper's daughter.'

The control room operator thought back to her conversation with Glenis earlier that morning and closed her eyes.

'Is she breathing?' she asked.

'I don't think so, no.'

'Can you double check for me, please, lovey?'

There was no reply but the control room operator did not require one to know the answer.

* * *

Jack Harris turned to walk over to his vehicle when his mobile phone rang. He fished the device out of his jacket pocket and glanced down at the readout. *DI Roberts*, it said. Something deep inside told him what she was about to say. Harris had felt increasingly uneasy in the days leading up to the council meeting but had not confided the reason to any of his colleagues. Never a man who found it easy to open up when it came to his emotions, even to those closest to him, the inspector had kept his feelings pent up. However, as he observed rising tension among the townsfolk of Levton Bridge, he had been assailed by a dark sense of foreboding. A sense that events were spiralling out of control. A sense that something was going to happen.

The others picked up on his anxiety and watched nervously as he took the call.

'Gillian,' said Harris. He tried to sound relaxed. 'I do hope this call is to tell me that young Annabelle Roper has turned up safe and sound and that I should not–'

'Sorry, Hawk,' said the detective inspector in the flat tones that she reserved for delivering bad news. 'I wish I could tell you that.'

'Where?'

'You're not going to like this,' said Gillian Roberts, 'but a woman walking her dog found her lying in the copse behind Rowan House. I've been out there and it's definitely Annabelle Roper. Sorry, Hawk, but it looks like Ellie Cross all over again.'

Harris looked back at County Hall, at the protestors, at David Roper, and at the television vans.

'There'll be no stopping them now,' he said.

Chapter four

'You look puzzled, Doc,' said Jack Harris.

'That's one word for it.' The white-haired Home Office pathologist frowned as he crouched over the body of Annabelle Roper, which was lying on its back in the copse. 'Disturbed would be another.'

'But it's straightforward, isn't it? Drugs? Just like Ellie Cross?'

'I think she's probably taken something like MDMA, yes, but in my experience, there is no such thing as a straightforward death. And as for it being like last time, come and see what you make of this, will you?' The pathologist gestured for the inspector to look closer. 'I'd appreciate your expert opinion.'

'My expert opinion?' Harris crouched down next to him. 'What am I looking at?'

The pathologist pulled up the girl's T-shirt to reveal livid scratch marks across her stomach.

'They're on her back as well. And here…' Doc reached over and rolled up the girl's left sleeve so that the detective could see more marks. 'On both arms, in fact. They're not injection marks.'

'Defensive wounds?'

'Not sure.' The pathologist frowned again. 'That's what is puzzling me, Hawk. Look, I know that this may sound crazy but, if I didn't know better, I'd say that those marks were done by an animal.'

'An animal?' Harris stared at him. 'What kind of animal?'

'Wildlife Liaison Officer is one of your duties, isn't it? You tell me but there's a real ferocity about them.'

'Not sure that any animal would do that, though.' Harris looked closer at the gashes and shook his head. 'No, definitely not.'

The inspector stood up and brushed the flecks of grass off his trousers. The pathologist remained beside the body, still staring pensively down at the marks.

'I don't know.' Doc shook his head. 'It just doesn't feel right.'

'Are you one hundred percent sure that they weren't done by a human being?'

'I'll only know when I do the post-mortem but you have to admit that they do look like claw marks,' said Doc. 'I am thinking that she died sometime between midnight and 3:00am – it's difficult to be precise with these warm summer nights – so I'm wondering if it could be a fox? Out and about, stumbles on the body and…'

'They're pretty catholic feeders, are foxes, but a human corpse?' Harris shook his head. 'And why would it attack her? They kill for food but there's no sign of feeding.'

'Maybe it was disturbed.'

'Sorry, can't see it, Doc, I really can't,' said the inspector. 'Are the scratch marks what killed her?'

'No, I suspect that your first instinct was right and that it *was* drug-related. However, the scratches do seem to indicate some kind of a struggle, do they not? Ellie Cross had nothing like that. All the evidence pointed to her having taken the drug of her own volition but I think Annabelle was forced to take it.'

'So it would seem,' said the detective.

'Sometimes, I despair of this world, Hawk. I've seen some things but force-feeding a kid drugs... it beggars belief what people will do to children.' The pathologist gestured to the scratches on the girl's arm then glanced up at the inspector. 'I mean, have you ever seen anything like it?'

'Not like this, no.'

The pathologist sensed something in the detective's voice and looked at him intently.

'Nothing?' he asked.

'I've seen dead kids, of course.'

The pathologist waited for Harris to elaborate but the inspector stayed silent. He always had. However, the detective *had* seen evidence of man's inhumanity towards children and, standing in the copse, a memory stirred deep within. Like all the other bad memories from his days in the Army, it had been suppressed for more than two decades, relentlessly forced back down whenever it threatened to bubble to the surface. A phone call a few days previously had made that increasingly difficult. The Army counsellor had told him all those years ago that he needed to bring the memories out into the open, had warned him that the day would come when something would trigger them back into life and that, when that happened, they would run out of control unless he talked them through with someone. Harris hadn't talked them through, had played the big man instead, like he always did. Now, more than twenty years later, he could not shake the thought that the phone call had proved the truth of her words and that he was paying the price.

1998. The Drenica region of Kosovo. Dusk in the dank forest. Murk creating grey shadows that danced in among the trees. A chill in the air. A heavy silence. No birds singing. Nothing stirring. And a growing sense among the soldiers that they were being watched. A deserted village, houses that had been torn apart then consumed by the flames as the homes were torched. Fifteen bodies sprawled on the damp grass, staring up at the leaden sky through sightless eyes. Mostly adults but among them four children. Three girls, one boy. None of them aged more than fourteen. One of them looked like she was not even ten years old. All had been butchered, their clothes caked in dried blood.

The group of soldiers from the United Nations peace-keeping force stood and stared wordlessly at the corpses. They were part of the team that had been sent to investigate the rumours of a massacre, to try to work out which of the sides in the bloody civil war had perpetrated such an outrage. Now, they were struck dumb, appalled by yet another example of the slaughter that had characterised the conflict. They had been warned about what they might find but even the most hardened among the group were unprepared for this.

'These memories will never leave us,' said the captain. His voice quivered with emotion as he thought of his two children back home in the UK, safe and warm in the family home. 'Never.'

Jack Harris said nothing. No one was surprised. The sergeant rarely ventured anything about what he was feeling. Besides, standing there he was not sure that the words existed to adequately express what any of them were experiencing. He was sure of one thing, though, that the captain was right when he said that they would always carry the memories with them.

Looking down at the body of Annabelle Roper, the memory of that dark day had forced its way to the surface once more, had risen so suddenly that he had not had time to force it down again. A voice cut into his reverie.

'You OK?' asked the pathologist.

Harris banished the image but he knew that it would not be for long.

'Yeah, sure,' he said. He returned his attention to the body. 'So, you're pretty sure that we're looking at a murder?'

'I reckon so.' The pathologist looked over towards the former Victorian villa that housed Rowan House, the roof only just visible over the high red-brick perimeter wall. 'If I'm right, that would give you a big problem, would it not?

A political one. I understand that this morning's council meeting was somewhat entertaining. Passions running high and a certain chief inspector stirring the pot.'

'You could say that.'

'They'll jump on this then,' said the pathologist. 'And please tell me it's a coincidence that the poor girl's name is Roper. It's not David's girl, is it?'

'I am afraid it is. Do you know him?'

'Only from Rotary.'

Before they could continue the conversation, Matty Gallagher pushed his way through the gate in the wall and walked towards them. The sergeant glanced down at the body.

'Same as the last one, Doc?' he asked. 'Overdose?'

'Not quite.' The pathologist pulled up the T-shirt again, to reveal the scratches across the stomach.

'Defensive wounds?' The sergeant gave a low whistle. 'Murder then?'

'Possibly,' said Harris. 'Anything useful from Rowan House?'

'Only that James Hall is being arsey. Says we can't interview any of his staff until he's talked to you. You can't see the copse from the house anyway.'

'So why's he being awkward?

'Seems to think that we're going to pin the girl's death on the centre. Wants "reassurances", whatever that means.'

'Not sure I can give him that, Matty lad. It's one hell of a coincidence.' Harris nodded towards the gate. 'I assume that the residents can use that to get here?'

'Not officially. It's supposed to be locked but one of the staff told me that they usually don't bother. He reckons that some of the boys come out here for a crafty smoke on an evening. The staff turn a blind eye. To be honest, things seem pretty lax.'

'Wonder what else they turn a blind eye to,' said Harris. 'Time to see our Mr Hall, I think, although I imagine that

I'm not exactly his favourite person after the council meeting.'

'That's under-stating it,' said Gallagher. 'He was calling you out something rotten. Public servant taking sides etc etc.'

'I'll bet he was.' The inspector reached down and helped the pathologist to his feet. 'I'll leave you to wrap up here, Doc.'

Doc grimaced as his arthritic knee protested.

'Don't get old,' he said. He winced and rubbed his leg. 'It's not all it's cracked up to be.'

'I'm not sure that Annabelle would agree,' said Harris. 'Let me know what the PM shows, will you? Particularly if you find evidence of a pack of hyenas roaming round Levton Bridge.'

'Hyenas?' asked Gallagher, looking bemused.

'I'll tell you later,' said Harris. 'Come on, let's go and see what James Hall has to say for himself.'

'Good luck,' said the pathologist. 'You'll need it with that one.'

'You know him as well?' asked Harris.

'Not well, but enough to know what he's like. He gave a talk on Rowan House to the Rotary Club the week before last. Don't quote me, but he's a self-opinionated pain in the derrière. Too full of himself, for my liking. And woe betide anyone who questions what he's doing at Rowan House.'

'Things kick off, did they?' asked Gallagher.

'Just a bit. A couple of the members tried to challenge him after the talk – one of them had been burgled a couple of nights previously and David Roper was the other one.' Doc looked down at the body. 'It was a few days after Annabelle spent the evening smoking cannabis with that Smedley lad. Roper tried to say it was Hall's fault.'

'He'll not have liked that,' said the sergeant.

'He certainly didn't. He slapped both of the guys down and refused to talk to anyone else. The speakers usually

29

stay for a drink and a chat but he couldn't get out fast enough. A nomination for an award and he thinks he's God's gift.'

Harris nodded gloomily and the detectives pushed their way through the gate and headed across the neatly manicured lawn towards Rowan House, leaving the pathologist and the forensic team to continue their examination of the scene.

'We're not looking at something straightforward then,' said the sergeant as they walked. 'You don't get injuries like that without putting up a fight.'

'Doc's pretty sure that she was force-fed drugs.'

'In which case, that County Lines operation with Northumbria can't happen soon enough. Two deaths in just over a month. Curtis will be demanding answers. Everyone will be demanding answers.'

'And they're right to do so,' said Harris.

The detectives stepped onto the paved path which led to the rear of the house. After taking a few paces, Harris stopped walking and looked at Gallagher.

'Did we miss something after Ellie died, do you think?' he asked.

Gallagher stopped walking as well.

'No, I don't think so,' he said. They started walking towards the house again. 'Mind, it didn't help that all the kids clammed up after it happened. I reckon that some of them know exactly what's been going on. There's got to be a good chance that Northumbria Police are right and that this new gang is shipping drugs over to our part of the world.'

'As it happens, I'm due to talk to their DCI this afternoon. You don't know Mel Garside, do you? Before your time maybe.'

'Heard of her by name. Went to their Organised Crime Unit, didn't she? A sharp operator, apparently.'

'As good as they come,' said Harris. 'Hopefully, she can firm up the link. Any sign of Smedley?'

'Uniform have got everyone out looking for him. He's always been an elusive one, has our Lee, though. Do you really think he's capable of murder?'

'I don't know, Matty lad. There's certainly something about him.' The inspector thought of the scratches and cast about for the correct phrase with which to describe the teenager. 'Something of the animal.'

'I know what you mean. You're never quite sure how he's going to react. But forcing drugs down a girl's throat, that takes a lot of believing.'

'You'd be amazed at what people can do. Even to children.'

'It's certainly not too big a leap for David Roper, from what I hear. According to the DI, he's convinced that Annabelle's death is down to Smedley. I said we'd go and see them when we're done here.'

'How are they?'

'Mum is in bits.'

'And Dad?'

'You saw him at County Hall,' said Gallagher. 'The DI says that the grief hasn't really kicked in yet and he's still looking for someone to blame. I think you can guess where he's going to start.'

The officers paused to listen to the shouting that was now emanating from the protestors who were gathering at the front gate at ever-growing numbers, watched warily by a small number of police officers. With the numbers swelling and the mood turning ever more menacing, the uniformed inspector in charge of the operation had already called for extra officers to prevent the protestors forcing their way into Rowan House.

'They didn't hang around, did they?' said Harris.

'Someone put a post on their Facebook page, apparently,' said Gallagher. 'Said that Annabelle had been found and that folks should head up here. Whoever it was, they said that we have a lot of questions to answer as well.

They're not going to miss an opportunity like this, are they?'

'Check out if it was this Ricky B character who posted it, will you? And get our techies to dig up anything they can about him. I want to know who he is and what his game is.'

'Will do.' Gallagher stopped walking again, took his smartphone from his coat pocket and called up Facebook. He scrolled down the page for a couple of moments. 'I appear to have done our Ricky B a disservice. Miriam Canley wrote the post.'

'If that woman wants trouble, she's going the right way about it.'

'It's a social media thing,' said Gallagher. 'People say all sorts of stuff online that they would never say face to face and it only needs someone to whip them for things to get out of hand.'

'You clearly don't know Miriam Canley,' grunted Harris. They walked into the house. 'She doesn't need someone blowing into her ear to cause trouble.'

Chapter five

After the detectives entered Rowan House, a worried-looking secretary ushered them along a corridor.

'Those people won't be able to get in, will they?' she said as the shouting from outside grew louder.

'We've got officers there to stop that happening,' said Gallagher.

A couple of loud thuds echoed from outside.

'Well, I hope there's enough of them,' said the secretary.

She ushered the detectives into James Hall's book-lined office. The manager exuded hostility from behind his desk as he watched Harris and Gallagher take their seats. Harris glanced at the bookshelves. Most of the titles appeared to be academic works on sociology. He looked back at Hall and sighed; the inspector had never coped well with theorists.

Hall noticed the gesture but said nothing, preferring instead to brood. In the heavy silence that followed, they could all hear the angry shouts coming from the direction of the front gate.

'I suppose you told them about this, did you?' said Hall. He looked accusingly at Harris. 'Part of your campaign to get us closed down, is it? If you can't get your way by official channels, you tip off the opposition? Is that it?'

'We did not tell them anything,' said Harris, bridling at the comment. 'And I'd thank you to credit us with some sense of–'

'Then perhaps you'd like to explain why they've turned up.'

'Social media,' said Gallagher quickly before the inspector could inflame the situation even further. The sergeant knew that his boss hated being interrupted. 'Someone posted something on Facebook.'

'And who did that?'

'Miriam Canley.'

'I might have known,' said Hall. 'Another bloody troublemaker. Well, however they found out, I imagine that they are going to make a big thing of this. They'll use it to blacken our name even further.'

'I imagine they will,' said Harris. 'Mind, it's hardly surprising that they think like that given the amount of incidents that have been linked to–'

'Yes, well you might as well know that I did not appreciate your comments this morning, Chief Inspector. In my view, public servants should not take sides. Their job is to be impartial.'

Gallagher held his breath; if there was one thing that the inspector detested more than being interrupted once, it was being interrupted twice – then being lectured. Hall, however, did not give Harris the chance to protest.

'Councillors find it difficult enough to understand our work as it is,' he continued. 'Between you and me, they're a bit simple, most of them, and the last thing we need is scaremongering contributions like yours. Such interventions can only further damage our reputation.'

'Is that all you can think of?' exclaimed Harris, unable to contain himself any longer. 'Your precious reputation!'

This time, Matty Gallagher could do nothing to prevent the outburst. Nor did he try. Instead, he sat back and let the conversation take its course. The sergeant had no desire to make things easier for James Hall; the manager's attitude had irritated him as well and if the man was unwise enough to take on Jack Harris…

'You may not value what we are doing here–' began Hall.

'In case you hadn't noticed,' said Harris, his turn to interrupt, 'there's a dead girl in your garden.'

'Not *in* our garden.'

'As near as makes no difference!' exclaimed Harris. 'That gate out the back? The sergeant tells me that it should be locked at night but that it never is. That you're pretty lax when it comes to security.'

'This is not a prison.'

'But it's supposed to be supervised,' said Harris. 'That's what we keep being told. Is it possible that one of your lads could have got out into the copse to meet Annabelle Roper last night?'

'I resent the implication that her death has to be something to do with our boys, Chief Inspector. In fact–'

'Just answer the question, Mr Hall.' Harris gave him a hard look. 'Could one of the boys have got out through that gate last night?'

'It's not the only way onto the field. The dog walkers are always walking across it. You can get onto it from the road. However, to answer your question, I am sure that none of our boys are involved in this and I object to the way you have immediately jumped to the conclusion that they are.'

'We are just trying to ascertain the truth,' said Harris. 'As for your precious boys, Annabelle Roper is the one you should be worrying about.'

Hall noted the anger flashing in the inspector's eyes, considered the comment and nodded.

'Yes, of course. It's a tragedy.' His words sounded false, delivered because he thought that they were what the detectives wanted to hear. 'Absolutely awful, and I have great sympathy for her family, of course I do, but you have to understand that I also have to think of the wellbeing of the boys who live here. People forget that they're still children. We haven't got anyone over sixteen here.'

'We'll be sure to tell Annabelle's parents that,' said Harris. 'I'm sure that it will prove to be a source of great comfort to them in the days to come, even though their daughter will never see sixteen.'

'Look, I do not wish to come over as uncaring,' said Hall. He realised that he needed to placate the irritated inspector and do it quickly; the man would make a powerful enemy, he'd already shown that at the council meeting. 'I know that our boys are not angels but, like it or not, it's my job to think of their interests. It's awful that a young girl has taken it on herself to take drugs—'

'And how do you know that?' asked Harris sharply. 'How do you know it was drugs?'

'I just assumed.' Hall was thrown by the detective's response. 'I mean, after what happened to that other girl. Ellie Cross.'

'Yes, well, in our line of work, we never assume anything, Mr Hall. In fact, we think that Annabelle may have been murdered.'

Hall stared at the detective in horror. Ramifications played out in his mind, none of them good. He thought of the councillors who had so narrowly voted to keep Rowan House open, thought of the fractious behind-the-scenes discussions that had threatened to derail everything ahead of the planning committee. Thought of the compromises Gerald Gault had been forced to make to win the support of his party colleagues.

It seemed to everyone in the room that the shouts from the protestors had grown louder.

'Murdered?' said Hall in a hollow voice. 'But I thought…'

'We suspect that she was forced to take drugs,' said Harris. 'Probably MDMA. Where's Lee Smedley?'

'Now, hang on. Surely, you don't think that Lee has anything to do with this?'

'Annabelle Roper told her pals that he was her boyfriend after that evening she spent with him and Danny,' said Gallagher. 'We already know that Lee deals in drugs and now she's dead and he's gone walkabout. Danny Cairns didn't do a runner so you can't blame us for suspecting that Lee Smedley is the one who was involved, can you? Doesn't take a genius to work it out, I would suggest.'

'Now who's making assumptions?' Hall instantly regretted the comment as Gallagher glared at him. 'I am sorry, Sergeant, that was uncalled for. I apologise.'

No point in making two enemies, thought the centre manager. The sergeant could turn out to be useful leverage in his dealings with Jack Harris, although his deepening scowl suggested that the damage may already have been done.

'Look,' continued Hall, trying to placate him, 'all I am saying is that, as far as I know, Lee only sells a bit of weed. I know that you have your reservations about cannabis, Chief Inspector, you made that abundantly clear at the council meeting this morning, but it's not exactly the hard stuff, is it? I mean, which of us didn't try it out when we were kids?'

'I didn't,' said Harris.

Gallagher's mind went back to a night in his teenage years in Bermondsey, memories of a spinning head and echoing voices and a terrible feeling the following morning as he tried to explain himself to the school nurse. Memories also of his father's baleful expression when his son was sent home by the headteacher and the sting of his hand across the teenager's cheek. Gallagher shook his head slightly to banish the memory and focused instead on the conversation.

'Where was Smedley between eleven at night and three in the morning?' asked Harris.

Hall hesitated.

'Well?' asked Harris. He fixed Hall with one of his looks. 'Was he here?'

'I don't think he was, no.'

'Hang on,' said Gallagher. 'Then how come one of your staff told Detective Constable Butterfield that he went to school this morning when she contacted you in connection with the burglary at Nightingale Road?'

The room was silent for a few moments, apart from the yelling of the protestors at the front gate. Hall seemed unsure about how best to respond.

'Well?' said Harris. 'If he didn't leave here for school this morning, where was he?'

'I don't know,' admitted Hall. 'All I know is that his bed had not been slept in.'

'So, why would your staff lie to us?' asked Gallagher. 'Why not just tell us the truth? That Lee Smedley was missing?'

'They probably didn't want to get him in any more trouble,' said Hall. 'Your officers are always on his back.'

'Are you surprised?' exclaimed Gallagher. 'The kid's a one-man crimewave but every time we try to get him locked up, he gets sent back here instead.'

'Yes, but we are trying to tackle the effects of the revolving–'

'If I hear one more thing about the bloody revolving door…' growled Harris. 'If you ask me, someone, somewhere is taking the piss when it comes to Lee Smedley. He should be locked up, not allowed to come and go as and when he pleases. He's a criminal and should be treated as one.'

'If I may say so, Chief Inspector, yours is an outdated point of view that reveals your lack of understanding of young people. Besides, we are making progress with Lee.'

'Are you hell as like!' exclaimed Harris. 'That increase in crime I mentioned at the meeting this morning? Most of it's down to Lee Smedley. And if it's not him, it's one of his cronies. Isn't that right, Sergeant?'

Gallagher nodded.

'Danny Cairns, most likely,' he said. 'Well, we'll want to talk to all of them.'

'Your officers talked to them when Ellie Cross died,' protested Hall. 'And they found nothing to connect any of our boys to the sale of MDMA. I can't see the point in repeating the exercise. Whoever supplied poor Annabelle Roper, it wasn't any of our lads.'

'We will still want to talk to them,' said Harris. He stood up. 'No ifs, no buts.'

'I'd rather you didn't. It could prove counter-productive.'

'Not as counter-productive as having your daughter lying dead in a wood.'

Hall considered the comment, again noted the fire in the inspector's eyes and gave a slight nod of the head. Like everyone in Levton Bridge, he knew that the detective had a temper on him. Time to play the game, he decided. No point in being on the wrong side of Jack Harris. Not yet anyway.

'You're right, of course, Chief Inspector,' he said. His tone was more conciliatory. Or was designed to sound so. 'I'm not thinking straight and I apologise. This has come as a great shock to all of us. Is there any way in which I can help?'

Harris sat down again, suspicious but partially mollified.

'You can start by telling us more about the relationship between Annabelle and Lee Smedley,' he said.

'I'm not sure it was that serious, really. There were a number of girls who kept coming here, wanting to see the boys. Young people who know them from Roxham Comprehensive. They meet in the copse sometimes.'

'Was Annabelle Roper one of them?' asked Harris.

'I don't know.'

'And did they meet last night?'

'I don't know that either. It's not every night. Maybe two or three times a week.'

'And you didn't stop it happening?'

'We certainly didn't encourage it but associating is not a crime, Chief Inspector.' Hall was unable to resist adding a barbed comment. 'Despite what the local constabulary may think.'

Harris stood up again and pointed a finger at the centre manager.

'You need to work out whose side you are on,' he said. 'Two young people are dead and I have this awful feeling that more might follow unless we do something about it. We'll not stop looking for Lee Smedley just because you think it's "counter-productive".'

Hall thought of the effect that increased police scrutiny would have on Rowan House. Time to give something up, he decided. Play the game.

'I understand that he has connections in Newcastle,' he said.

'Connections?' said Harris. 'What sort of connections?'

'I have no more information than that, I am afraid. Just something one of the staff said. I can't recall who it was.'

'It's useful enough.' Harris glanced at Gallagher, who nodded. 'If Smedley comes back, I want to know the moment he appears. And I want my officers to be afforded the fullest co-operation by you and your staff. I don't want to hear that anyone is trying to protect the boys. This is a murder inquiry and you'd do well to remember it.'

Hall looked as if he was about to remonstrate with the inspector but one look at the set of the detective's jaw, then at Gallagher's impassive expression, persuaded him to think better of it.

'Of course,' he said.

'If Smedley hasn't gone to Newcastle, any idea where else he might be?' asked Gallagher.

'Sometimes in the summer he spends the night outside. He's read a lot of books on survival skills. He's absolutely fascinated with it, they're just about the only books he reads. He wants to go in the Army when he's old enough.'

'Well, he's not doing his chances much good,' said Harris. The inspector paused with his hand on the door handle and looked back at the centre manager. 'One other thing. Do you get any trouble with foxes round here?'

Hall looked surprised.

'Foxes?' he said. 'What's that—'

'Just answer the question. Do you?'

'They've been spotted round the bins from time to time. We had a couple last week, I think. After chicken bones, I believe. The staff chased them off.'

Harris did not reply but walked out of the room, followed by a bemused Gallagher who caught him up in the corridor.

'Why did you ask that?' said the sergeant.

'Something the Doc said. We didn't know that Lee Smedley had connections in Newcastle, did we?'

'No, we reckoned they were all back in Blackpool where his mum lives. However, if it's true, that brings him well and truly into the County Lines investigation, doesn't it?'

'Big time,' said Harris. 'Perhaps we dismissed the idea that he was their runner too quickly. I told you that we'd missed something, Matty lad. I'll run it past Mel Garside when I speak to her this afternoon.'

As the officers neared the front door, they heard the shouts from the protestors growing ever louder as their numbers continued to increase. Harris opened the door and scowled as he saw a television van pull up. The inspector knew that it would not be the last one to arrive.

Chapter six

Such a stark contrast, thought Jack Harris as he and Matty Gallagher sat and surveyed Annabelle Roper's parents in the living room of their home, a large newly built detached house on the edge of Levton Bridge. Never particularly given to empathy when it came to people, Harris knew enough to realise that it was unwise to jump to conclusions when dealing with victims. Grief, he reflected, always affected people in dramatically different ways. The inspector had been thinking a lot about grief in recent days, ever since the phone call had stirred up unwelcome memories of that day in the forest clearing in Kosovo.

Grief certainly had affected David and Glenis Roper in different ways. Annabelle's mother was crushed. Sitting on the sofa next to Alison Butterfield, she clutched a sodden handkerchief, her eyes red-rimmed, tears creating rivers on her cheeks, her life torn apart by a moment of violence. Her husband, on the other hand, was sitting upright in a chair, his knuckles glowing white as he gripped the arms, his features etched with anger, his eyes bright with fury. David Roper was a man who was lashing out, a man in search of revenge for the death of his beloved daughter, a man who was determined that someone should pay and woe betide anyone who stood in his way.

Harris briefly wondered how the families of the children who had perished in the forest clearing had reacted all those years ago in Kosovo. Assuming that any of them had been left alive. With a jolt, he realised, perhaps for the first time, that he did not even know their names. The inspector inwardly rebuked himself for allowing the thought to force its way to the surface; he had to keep his mind on the job. And that meant dealing with David Roper's fury.

'I want that boy arrested,' said Roper. He jabbed a finger at Harris. 'I want Lee Smedley found and strung up from the nearest—'

'We don't know for definite that it's him.'

'Of course it's him! He's the little shit who pestered our daughter and I want him—'

'Please, David,' pleaded Glenis. She gave her husband a beseeching look. 'Not now.'

'What do you mean, not now?' Roper glared at her. 'If not now, when? Our daughter would still be alive if the police had done their job properly. That toerag has been allowed to run round this town—'

'I appreciate that you feel—' began the inspector.

'Oh, don't give me that slaver! Your lot have had plenty of opportunity to do something about Lee Smedley. You knew what he was like! Preying on the innocent, breaking into people's houses, selling our kids drugs. Now you tell us that you think he might have forced Annabelle to take drugs. How the hell am I supposed to react?'

'I didn't say that, Mr Roper,' replied Harris calmly. 'All I said was that we would like to speak to him.'

'Yes, and I know what that means. Why was he allowed to give Annabelle the drugs?' Roper glared at the detective. 'Answer me that, Chief Inspector.'

'It's complicated.' Harris was acutely aware that it sounded like a lame response, knew that he had been asking himself the same question over and over again since the discovery of the body, that there was nothing complicated about the reply. He, the police, the courts, the system, had all failed the Ropers and many other people in Levton Bridge. End of.

'Complicated!' exclaimed Roper. 'God knows how many times you have arrested him, and what have you achieved? Nothing. Absolutely bloody nothing! He should have been locked up long before he had a chance to do this to our daughter.'

'I admit it's not a perfect system—'

'Not perfect! You've been listening to the rubbish that James Hall spouts. Bloody do-gooders!'

Anger spent, Roper slumped back in the chair. Tears glistened in his eyes and his lower lip started to quiver as the enormity of what had happened had overwhelmed him and grief finally forced its way to the surface. The detectives gave him time to recover his composure.'

'I'm sorry for having a go at you,' said Roper eventually. His voice was quieter now. 'It's just that…'

His voice tailed off and he struggled to retain his composure.

'We can't imagine what the two of you are going through,' said Harris. He tried to sound sympathetic, always an effort. 'I know it's difficult for you both but we have to ask you some questions. We have to find out how Annabelle came to be in the copse. We need to make sure that this does not happen to any more of our young people.'

Both parents nodded. Glenis looked out of the window at the rain drizzling across the neatly manicured lawn. Her tears welled again. David Roper tried hard to hold onto his composure but Harris could see that the anger was bubbling up again.

'You said that Lee Smedley pestered your daughter,' said the inspector. 'However, we were told after she went missing last time that they were going out together.

44

Annabelle was telling people that she was Lee's girlfriend. James Hall doubts whether it's true but–'

'It's the first sensible thing the man has said. I told your officers that last time. There's no way that Annabelle would want anything to do with someone like Smedley. He's an animal and she was an angel.'

Finally, his emotions got the better of him.

'An absolute angel,' he said through the tears.

* * *

'Annabelle Roper?' smirked the shaven-headed young man sitting across the desk from Detective Constable Alistair Marshall. 'She was a right slag, she was.'

'Nothing like respect for the dead,' said Marshall. 'I'm sure you can complete the sentence yourself.'

It was early afternoon and the constable and Danny Cairns were at Roxham Comprehensive School, sitting in a room that had been set aside for interviews. Marshall had already spent an hour and a half talking to the dead girl's closest friends and now had moved onto the wider circle of acquaintances. Danny Cairns' presence the last time she vanished made him a person of great interest. He was also part of the group of teenagers often seen around Levton Bridge marketplace on evenings and sometimes in the copse behind Rowan House, where he was a resident, smoking and drinking cheap strong cider. Annabelle Roper had occasionally been seen with them.

'Tell the truth, you said.' Cairns gave a smile that revealed yellowed, crooked teeth. 'So, I'm telling you the truth. Folks may not want to hear it, but she was right up for it, was Annabelle Roper. Her and her pals.'

'Are you sure?' asked Marshall. 'You're not just repeating gossip, are you? Stringing me a line? See, that's not the impression that we're getting of her.'

'I'll bet it's not. Her parents thought that she was some kind of angel but, you can take it from me, she wasn't.' Cairns gave another smirk. 'I know what you're thinking,

45

what do nice girls like them want with toerags like me and Lee? But it was her who told people that she was Lee's girlfriend. He never said it. She made all the running.'

'I'm still not sure I believe you, Danny.'

'Believe what you want but these posh girls like their fun. Ellie Cross was the same. Butter wouldn't fucking melt but give them a spliff…'

Marshall gave him a sharp look. Neither the names of Lee Smedley nor Danny Cairns had featured in the investigation into the death of the teenager. As far as the police knew, Ellie Cross was not in their circle of friends.

'And how do you know that Ellie Cross smoked cannabis?' asked the constable. 'All we said publicly was that she had died from a bad reaction to MDMA.'

For the first time in the interview, Cairns looked uncomfortable. Wary. He glanced away.

'Well?' said Marshall. 'How come you know so much about Ellie Cross?'

'I don't, really. Just saw her around school, you know. Just to look at. Never spoke to her, like.'

'Then why mention her?' asked the detective. 'Why say that she liked her fun?'

'Just what I'd heard.'

'Heard from whom?' Marshall leaned forward in his seat. 'Not from Lee Smedley, by any chance?'

'No comment.'

'We don't do no comment, son.' The detective had learned the phrase from Harris and intensified his stare, another of the inspector's tricks. 'How well did you know Ellie Cross, Danny? Was she one of the girls you and Lee knocked around with? Maybe you saw her at Rowan House? Maybe you know more about her death than you're letting on. Come on, the truth, this time.'

'I had nowt to do with what happened to her, if that's what you're thinking. None of us did.'

'Nevertheless, you clearly know much more than you are letting on,' said Marshall. Come on, Danny, this could be important. Two of your fellow pupils are dead. You don't want it to happen to anyone else, surely?'

'I ain't no grass.'

Cairns looked away again and the ensuing silence allowed Marshall to think back to the evening when he had first heard the name Ellie Cross. He was the duty CID officer when the call came in to Levton Bridge Police Station shortly after 11:00pm; a fifteen-year-old had been found dead at the detached family home in the upmarket end of town. Marshall recalled how he had looked down at the body sprawled on the bed. He'd seen bodies before, of course he had, but her age had stirred something deep inside him; for God's sake, she was only nine years younger than he was.

In the days that followed, detectives discovered from her friends that the MDMA had been supplied by someone she knew. However, the teenagers had been unable to provide officers with the name. Or unwilling. If her friends did know anything, they weren't telling. Wall of silence. Which was when Mel Garside had contacted Harris to report that their County Lines operation in Newcastle had thrown up a possible link with the valley. A runner, someone taking drugs from the city to the valley. 'This could be bigger than we think,' Harris had said at a briefing in the squad room a few days after the death of Ellie Cross.

Now, noticing that Cairns was looking at him uneasily, Marshall returned his attention to the job at hand.

'I asked you a question, Danny,' he said. 'I'll ask it again. What do you know about Ellie Cross?'

Cairns looked increasingly uncomfortable and the detective tried to contain his growing excitement at the prospect of a breakthrough. This was a chance to impress Jack Harris, and the ambitious young detective knew it.

'Well?' said Marshall as the silence lengthened.

The teenager shook his head.

'I've already said too much,' he said. 'It's more than my life's worth to say owt else.'

'You do know that Jack Harris is heading this inquiry, don't you? I mean, you have heard of Jack Harris, haven't you?' Marshall smiled slightly at the teenager's worried expression. 'You do know what he's like when he thinks people are jerking his chain?'

'Lee hates him. Says he's a bully.'

'Well, you'll have cause to hate him as well if I have to go back and tell him that you are withholding information.' Marshall lowered his voice, tried to sound more sympathetic. Like he understood. 'Come on, Danny. Where can we find Lee Smedley?'

'No comment. Jack Harris or not, I ain't saying nowt.'

Marshall sighed; it had been the same story throughout an increasingly frustrating day for the young detective. Every time he thought that he was getting somewhere, his hopes had been dashed. It felt like a re-run of Ellie Cross. All the pupils to whom he had talked had been loath to co-operate; even though they were shocked at the news about Annabelle, it was clear to the detective that the young people of Levton Bridge were determined to hold onto their secrets.

Realising that he was getting nowhere, the detective constable dismissed Danny Cairns and the teenager had just left the room when a slim, dark-haired young woman walked in. Marshall smiled a welcome at Angie Coulson; he had come to know and like the English teacher in the weeks following the death of Ellie Cross. Indeed, the constable had been plucking up courage to ask her out.

Professionally, Angie had been an important part of his enquiries in the weeks since the death of Ellie Cross. Now, she had assumed even more importance because, in addition to being an English teacher, she was the form tutor for a class that had included Annabelle Roper as well as Danny Cairns and Tracey Malham, both of whom had been with the teenager the last time she disappeared. Part of Angie's job was to oversee student welfare and the constable sensed that she was as frustrated as he was at the lack of progress in the investigation.

'How's it going?' she asked.

'It's not.'

She sat down at one the desks and shook her head. She was close to tears.

'It's a terrible thing,' she said quietly. 'You try to keep them safe but…'

'I'm sure you did your best,' said Marshall.

She shot him a grateful look.

'Thank you,' she said. 'You're still looking for Tracey Malham, I think?'

'I am. She turned up yet?'

'I am afraid not, Alistair. It appears that she's done a bunk.'

'A bunk?'

'Yes. Seems to have gone not long after she told me that she knew nothing about what happened to Annabelle. She went to her first class but one of her friends reckons that she left the school grounds when she realised you still wanted to talk to her.'

'What's she hiding, do you think?' asked Marshall. 'Was last night a re-run of the first time they went missing together?'

'I don't know.'

'Did the friend know?'

The teacher raised an eyebrow.

'No, of course not,' said Marshall. He slapped his head in mock frustration. 'Silly me. Perish the thought that the young people of the area might actually want to co-operate with the police.'

'You not getting far, I take it, then?' She walked over to sit on the edge of the table. 'No one giving you any information?'

'Some are but, if you ask me, they're giving me stuff that they are pretty certain I already know.' Marshall sighed. 'Nope, the kids at this school just don't want to talk, Angie. You heard nothing new, I take it?'

'Just the usual gossip. That there's plenty of drugs around, if you know who to ask. Cannabis mainly, according to the kids. Is it true what I heard? That someone force-fed Annabelle MDMA?'

'Where did you hear that?'

'It's all over the school. You know what the rumour mill is like in these places. Is it true?'

'We believe so, yes. Look, Angie, I know it's a sensitive subject but are there any names that you can give me for kids who might be dealing in the stuff? I mean, you must hear things in your welfare role.'

'You know the rules, Alistair.' She stood up and headed for the door. 'What the kids tell me is confidential. I keep telling you that.'

'I know but this is a murder investigation now, Angie. That must change something?'

'I appreciate that but, for what it's worth, I haven't heard anything, no.'

'How about Lee Smedley?' asked Marshall as she reached for the door handle. 'Are you hearing anything new about him? And what about Danny Cairns?'

Angie turned and gave him a look.

'Just leave it, will you?' she said.

Just for a second, a fleeting second, she sounded frightened. However, it only lasted a second and, thinking back on it later, Marshall decided that he had imagined it anyway.

'OK, OK,' said the detective. He held up his hands in mock surrender. 'I get the message, miss.'

'They're not bad kids, you know.' She closed the door and walked back into the room. 'It's just that some of them have troubled backgrounds and are at a difficult age.'

'You really care about them, don't you?'

She nodded.

'Lads like Lee and Danny remind me of my childhood,' she said. 'My father left us when I was nine and I've not seen him since; my mum went to pieces, doped up on tranquilisers half the time. I ran the household, really.'

'Tough.'

'It was, but I'm evidence that if you give these kids a chance, they can make something of their life. Do you know, Alistair, I was the first person in my family to go university? My mum was so proud.'

'I'm sure she was.' Marshall sensed an easing of the tension. 'Tell me about Annabelle.'

'You never give up, do you? Always asking questions.'

'My governor wouldn't let me give up. I only met Annabelle once and even then not for long. But she hasn't got a tough background, has she?'

'Being a teenager is tough for all kids,' said Angie.

'So, what was she like?'

'Her dad described her as an angel.'

'And you?' asked the constable. 'How would you describe her? See, I've heard some things.'

'I'm sure you have, Alistair, but you know what kids are like – they say some daft stuff.'

'You didn't answer the question. What was she like?'

'I'll have to say the same thing as her dad says, won't I?' She gave a slight smile. 'After all, David Roper is a school governor. He must be right.'

Marshall nodded. As she walked into the corridor, he plucked up the courage to say what he had been wanting to say for weeks.

'I don't suppose you fancy going for a drink one night, do you?' he said.

She walked back into the room and a slight smile played on her lips.

'A date?' she asked.

'Yeah.'

'I don't think it's a good idea, given everything that's been going on, do you?'

The detective shook his head.

'No, I guess not,' he said.

'Maybe when things have settled down.'

Angie walked back into the corridor, leaving Alistair Marshall alone with his thoughts.

'Yeah, maybe,' he said.

After a few moments, the constable glanced up at the clock on the wall and sighed; an hour to go until hometime. He'd give it a bit longer before he rang Harris. Keep hoping for that breakthrough.

* * *

David Roper ushered Harris and Gallagher to the front door.

'You will get him, won't you?' he said. He gripped onto the inspector's arm. 'I know James Hall tries to say that the boys at Rowan House are only children but don't listen to him. Lee Smedley is an animal.'

Harris thought back to the scratches on Annabelle's body.

'I fear,' he said, 'that you may be right.'

* * *

By the time the Levton Bridge detectives had made the connection between the boys of Rowan House and Annabelle Roper, Lee Smedley was already long gone. Having spent the previous evening moving from place to place to avoid police patrols, he had slept rough behind the gardener's shed in the park for a few snatched hours, then caught the early bus out of town, breathing easier as the vehicle headed east across the moors, every rotation of the vehicle's wheels taking him further away from Levton Bridge.

By mid-morning, he was in Newcastle, where he caught another bus before disembarking in front of a row of shops on the edge of one of the city's sprawling housing estates. He was greeted by a short-haired man in his thirties, wearing jeans and a T-shirt depicting a leering skull, with a black cap jammed onto his head and a scar across one cheek. Rad surveyed Smedley's dishevelled appearance without much enthusiasm; the teenager's hair was lank and his cheeks were streaked with grime, but the eyes were sharp and bright as ever, constantly flicking left and right as if in search of danger. As ever, Rad felt unease. He tried to conceal his apprehension with a stern look.

'You had better not have been followed,' he said.

'Don't worry, I wasn't,' said Smedley. 'Just thought it was better to be out of the way for a while. The police are all over the fucking place.'

'Yeah, well you had better have had nothing to do with this kid's death.'

'It's fine,' said Smedley. 'I ain't got nothing to do with that.'

Rad looked sceptical but Smedley gave him a nod of reassurance and within moments they had disappeared into the urban jungle.

Chapter seven

Jack Harris had not long been back in his office in the Victorian building that housed Levton Bridge Police Station when his mobile phone rang. The inspector glanced at the readout and took the call.

'Alistair,' he said. 'Please tell me that you're getting somewhere.'

'I wish I could,' said the detective constable. 'The kids are a bit more forthcoming than last time but not much. Danny Cairns reckons Annabelle was nothing like the angel her dad says she was but he clammed up when I pressed him. Oh, and Tracey Malham has gone missing.'

'Has she now? You think she's involved?'

'She *was* with Annabelle last time.'

'She was indeed,' said Harris. He hesitated. 'Do you think we should be worried about her?'

'Difficult to tell with Tracey, guv. She's a law to herself, that one, but she knows how to look after herself. More street-wise than either Annabelle or Ellie were, I'd say.'

'You got people out looking for her?'

'Uniform are checking on her usual haunts and Alison looked in on her home but there's no one in and the neighbours weren't much use.'

'OK, keep me informed,' said Harris. 'I want her caught asap. I'm getting sick and tired of kids playing games with us.'

'Righto, guv.'

The line went dead just as a slim, balding uniformed officer walked into the room. As he always did, Philip Curtis frowned when he noticed the inspector's dogs slumbering beneath the radiator. Although the divisional commander's relationship with Harris had improved dramatically following a difficult start, the presence of the detective's mongrels in the station remained one of their disagreements. Curtis knew, however, that he had to pick his fights wisely with the irascible chief inspector and that Scoot and Archie were popular with the staff. Besides, he thought as he sat down, this was a time for unity. The pressure was on and the commander's phone had not stopped ringing since the discovery of Annabelle Roper's body.

'More trouble?' he asked. He gestured towards the mobile phone in the inspector's hand.

'Tracey Malham has gone missing.'

'We worried?'

'I've been worried ever since Ellie Cross died.'

'Yes, me, too.' Curtis took a seat. 'Any other updates? God knows, we could do with something positive. I'm getting a lot of heat from just about everyone, not least the chief's office.'

'And rightly so.'

Harris knew that he was in no position to object to what he usually saw as interference from headquarters. You couldn't argue with two dead teenagers in little over a month and well the inspector knew it. Particularly when at the back of his mind, there still nagged the uncomfortable suspicion that Annabelle Roper was only dead because the police had failed to make enough progress following the death of Ellie Cross.

'So, what do I tell the chief?' asked Curtis. 'What do I tell the media, for that matter? The press office has been bombarded with calls from journalists demanding more information, we've had dozens of calls from worried parents and I've just come off the phone with James Hall.'

'Complaining about me?'

'You're certainly not his favourite person – he said you were somewhat brusque with him – but no, it was about the number of television vans parked outside Rowan House. The protestors seem to be giving them plenty of footage to go at.'

'They certainly know how to play the media. We are pretty sure that someone is deliberately fomenting things. There were one or two people we didn't recognise. Matty is trying to put names to faces.'

'You thinking that someone from outside is stirring it?' asked Curtis.

'Possibly.'

'But surely it's just a local issue?'

'Maybe it's not. Maybe there's more to it than we realise. Matty's trying to identify a lad on Facebook by the name of Ricky B who keeps uploading inflammatory posts. Whoever they are, the death of Annabelle Roper has played right into their hands.'

'Which is why we need to get something positive out,' said the commander. 'Take some of the emotion out of the situation. Are we anywhere near arresting the Smedley kid?'

'Not yet and, when we do, we'll have to be careful how we phrase it if we tell the media. We have nothing definite to link him to the girl's death as yet.'

'But you're sure it's him?' said Curtis.

'Not one hundred percent.'

'Her father is.'

'How do you know that?'

'He rang me. One of the television reporters referred to the relationship in a piece to camera. She didn't mention

Smedley by name but said that the girl may have been going out with someone from Rowan House. David Roper was furious, demanding that we get her to retract the statement.'

'And how come *he* rang you, may I ask?' asked Harris suspiciously.

'Relax, it's nothing sinister. We know each other from Rotary. In fact, we were both there when James Hall gave his talk a few weeks back. Roper tried to ask a couple of questions afterwards – he was trying to blame Rowan House for letting Smedley lead his daughter astray.'

'According to Alistair Marshall, she was doing a pretty good job of it herself,' said Harris.

'Well, David Roper was having none of it. James Hall gave as good as he got, mind. He's not the type to brook anything he thinks may be criticism.' The commander gave Harris a sly look. 'I'm surprised that the two of you don't get on better.'

Harris allowed himself a slight smile in return. In the early days following the commander's appointment, he might have taken the comment personally but now he saw it for what it was – an attempt by the senior officer to use humour to keep his head of CID onside at difficult times. Harris appreciated the gesture; he was going to need all the friends he could get.

'Let's just say that myself and James Hall have a somewhat different outlook on life,' said Harris.

'Well, he didn't like your comments at the council meeting. I told him that you can't argue with the crime statistics.'

Harris nodded his approval.

'And Roper?' he said. 'What did you say to him?'

'That until we can prove that his daughter was not going out with Lee Smedley, we'll not be saying anything on the subject.'

'Very wise. I had hoped that Annabelle's death might loosen a few tongues but it would appear not.' Harris shook his head. 'I don't mind admitting that I am well out of my comfort zone. I don't understand teenagers.'

'Wait till you have some of your own,' said Curtis. 'There's one other thing. Emotions are running high and you're going to have to keep on top of it, so make sure that none of your team loses their head and does something silly. Child murders can do that to people, you know.'

Harris nodded. He thought of Annabelle Roper in the copse. Thought of the bodies lying in the forest clearing. Felt once again the chill of a Kosovan winter. Faces. Sightless eyes. Twisted limbs. Torn flesh.

'I know,' he said. 'I was thinking the same thing.'

The commander had only just left the room when Gallagher walked in to find Harris standing at the window, staring down moodily into the yard. The sergeant waited for a few seconds but still Harris did not acknowledge his presence.

'Guv?' he said eventually.

Harris turned round.

'Sorry,' he said. 'Didn't hear you come in.'

'You OK?'

'Yeah, sure.' Harris noticed the sergeant's concerned expression. 'Fine.'

The inspector sat down behind his desk and gestured to the computer print-out in Gallagher's hand.

'What's that then?' he asked.

Gallagher slid the paper across the table.

'Our techies checked out that Facebook account I mentioned,' he said. 'We were right about Ricky B not being on the level. It appears that he's one Jason Craig. Purports to live in Newcastle.'

'Purports?'

'You know what these Facebook types are like.'

'Not really,' said Harris.

'It's a fake address, like I suspected. They often are on Facebook. Our techies say that they cannot find anything to connect him to Levton Bridge, though.'

'So, what's he doing stirring things up here then?'

'Now there's a question,' said Gallagher.

* * *

Shortly after 2:30pm, three protestors broke through the police cordon that was guarding the front gate at Rowan House and sprinted up the drive towards the building to a chorus of cheers from the gathering. Officers quickly apprehended two of the young men, wrestling them to the ground amid shouts of condemnation from the protestors. However, the third man, who was dressed in jeans and a scuffed parka, struggled free from their grasp and continued to run up the front drive. As he neared the building, he gave a yell, produced a half-brick from inside his coat and hurled it at the house. The missile shattered the office window, showering glass over the terrified secretary who was sitting at her desk.

Another huge cheer went up from the crowd and the young man turned and punched the air in exultation before officers arrested him and walked him, with some difficulty, back down the drive towards one of their vehicles. He continued to struggle and angry cries emanated from the crowd as one of the officers twisted his arm behind his back so hard that he squealed in pain.

Standing by another of the police vans, the uniformed inspector in charge of the operation eyed the protestors uneasily. He did not recognise the three men who had been arrested but he did recognise most of the other faces as belonging to local people and he was shocked to see how the volatile atmosphere had transformed normally law-abiding townsfolk into baying members of the mob.

'This is getting out of hand,' he said. The inspector gestured to a young constable standing nearby. 'Put a call into the station, will you? See if Jack Harris is prepared to come down here? Maybe he can do something. Put his diplomatic skills to use.'

'What, Jack Harris diplomatic?'

'Yeah, the protestors like him after what he said at the meeting this morning.'

Another loud cry went up from the crowd.

'Not sure his approach is likely to help,' said the constable.

'On the contrary. Didn't you know that he was a hostage negotiator when he was in the Army? Kosovo, I think.'

'Was he?' The constable looked sceptical. 'You sure we're talking about the same Jack Harris?'

'I am indeed.' The inspector gave a slight smile. 'See, Constable, you think you know someone…'

Chapter eight

Harris had only just put his jacket on and started heading for the office door when his desk phone rang. He sighed, sat back down and took the call.

'Heard you've got a few problems over there,' said a woman's voice. 'Do you need some help from the big boys and girls in the city?'

'Just a bit,' said Harris. He had cheered up when he realised who it was. 'I need to get things moving, Mel. Calm things down.'

'I'll do what I can.'

Harris gave a slight smile. He had always liked Mel Garside and had been sad to see her leave her uniform post at Levton Bridge for a role as a detective chief inspector with the Northumbria force in her native Newcastle. Not that the move ended their contact; travelling crime had long been an issue in the valley and Harris regularly liaised with colleagues in neighbouring forces. He was pleased to do so with Garside. Harris was a simple man when it came to judging colleagues; if they got on with the job and didn't play games, he could work with them.

'So, what exactly do you have over there?' asked Garside. 'The Sky TV girl kept hinting that it might be a murder?'

'We think so, yes. Looks like Annabelle Roper was force-fed drugs. Doc reckons it was probably MDMA.'

'The reporter said that the body was found near Rowan House. Plenty of placard-waving, from what I could see.'

'Uniform reckon there's fifty or sixty of them at least. We think that someone from outside may be stirring things up.'

'Any idea why?' asked Garside.

'Not yet. Does the name Ricky B mean anything to you?'

'Sorry.'

'How about Jason Craig?' asked Harris. 'We think they're the same person.'

'Ah, now that does ring a bell,' said Garside. 'He cropped up in the early days of our investigation, I think. Can't quite remember why, though. He's certainly not anything big in our County Lines gang. I'll do some checking for you, though. You got anyone in the frame for the murder?'

'One of the Rowan House boys. Lad called Lee Smedley. He's gone missing.'

'Didn't you ask us to look at him over County Lines?'

'Yeah, we did,' said Harris. 'We wondered if he may be running the stuff from Newcastle over here but the name meant nothing to you.'

'I seem to recall that you thought he was more likely to be getting his drugs from Blackpool way?'

'That's where he's from. Lived there till he was fourteen. Dad buggered off when he was four, mum was a druggie who worked as a pro on the seafront.'

'Presumably wearing a *Kiss Me Quick* hat.'

'Do something quickly,' said Harris.

Garside gave a low laugh.

'So how did he end up in Levton Bridge?' she asked.

'Got sent here by the juvenile court. He attacked a kid after they'd been sniffing solvents and the court referred him to Rowan House to get him away from bad influences. We thought he was only selling a bit of weed but I'm wondering if we have underestimated him. We've just found out that he has Newcastle connections.'

'Sounds interesting. What do you need me to do?'

'I'm under a lot of pressure. It would really help if you could bring forward your operation. Show that we're not sitting on our hands.'

'Ideally, I'd have liked a couple of extra weeks to top and tail things but we can go early if it helps. How do you fancy having breakfast with me tomorrow?'

'Temptress.'

'On second thoughts, perhaps I had better rephrase that,' said Garside. 'Leckie tells me that you're still going out with that nice young blonde DI from Greater Manchester.'

'How come you've been talking to Leckie?'

'There's a link between our gang and Manchester and GMP want in on our op. See you tomorrow? Say 5:00am?'

'Fine. And thanks, Mel. You're digging me out of a hole.'

'No problem.'

Harris ended the call, stood up and headed for the door, dogs at his heels. He had just stepped into the corridor when his desk phone rang again.

'Leave me alone!' exclaimed the inspector. He went back over to the desk and picked up the receiver. 'DCI Harris.'

'It's Doc,' said the pathologist's voice. 'You asked for a cause of death on Annabelle Roper. She did die of a heart attack after taking MDMA. However, there are differences to Ellie Cross; I'd say that the MDMA that Annabelle took was deliberately mixed in with all sorts of nasties, including fentanyl. I'll send you a full breakdown.'

'Still murder then?'

'It's difficult to believe that whoever put it together was unaware of the damage it could cause but that's where it gets complicated, I am afraid. See, I pulled a few strings with the DNA bods as well so they've done a quick turnaround. Those scratch marks on her body? You were right, they weren't an animal. Definitely human.'

'Lee Smedley?'

'Who knows? Whoever it was is not on record and we don't have Smedley's DNA anyway. Sorry, old pal, not sure how much more help I can be at this stage, not until you arrest him.'

'Thanks, anyway.'

Just as Harris ended the call, a uniformed officer walked into the room.

'This has better be good,' said the inspector. 'I've been trying to get out for a slash for twenty minutes. And I'm not in the mood for any more bad news.'

'I'm not sure I'm going to help much then. The inspector's been on from Rowan House. Wonders if you'd like to get down there and have a word with the protestors? Things are getting a bit tasty. Some young hoodlum has just thrown a brick through a window.'

'Why me?'

'They think you're on their side after what you said at the council meeting.'

'But I told them I wasn't.'

'You try persuading Miriam Canley,' said the uniformed officer. 'She loves you, all of a sudden.'

Harris sighed; it was turning into one of those days.

Chapter nine

Jack Harris parked his mud-spattered white Land Rover in the leafy residential road near Rowan House, told the dogs to stay in the back, and got out of the vehicle. For a few moments, he stood and surveyed the angry crowd as the cordon of police officers struggled to hold the protestors back from the main gates. The inspector sighed and switched his attention to the view beyond the house, the hills with their summits shrouded in cloud, the lower slopes in shadow cast by the sun. As so often on such occasions, he longed to be up on the high moors, the dogs at his heels as they picked their way along the paths winding through the heather.

As the inspector stared at the hills, his mind drifted back to the conversation with James Hall and an image of a figure came to mind, a young man, strong, lean and lithe, running long and easy across the heather, his feet hardly touching the ground. A man at home on the tops. As the figure came nearer, the inspector could see that it was Lee Smedley. The detective frowned; the thought that, different as they may be, the two of them shared a love of his beloved hills disturbed him. He gave a shake of the head to banish the thought. Never a prosaic man, the idea had reinforced his growing view that something did not feel right, that his thoughts were not his own. He'd been feeling it ever since the phone call had revived memories of what happened in Kosovo.

Harris returned his attention to the protest. Watching the struggle at the gates to Rowan House, he shook his head again. He could not believe what he was seeing. The campaign had largely been conducted in a respectful manner over recent months but the day's events had suggested a change in approach, a harder edge, and Jack Harris did not like what he was witnessing. He knew that such heightened emotions in a small town could be damaging and, if left unchecked, could threaten the delicate balance that kept remote communities functioning peaceably.

The police tactic devised by Philip Curtis had been to keep a watching brief and allow the democratic process to run its course. Harris had agreed but the day's events were forcing the police's hand. He scanned the faces in the crowd. As with the scene outside County Hall, most of the protestors were people he recognised, respectable law-abiding townsfolk, but some of them he could not place. In particular, he honed in on a couple of young men in jeans and leather jackets who were hurling obscenities at the police. He recognised them from outside County Hall; he was sure there had been another young man with them. He wondered if it was Jason Craig.

The uniformed inspector walked over to Harris, breaking into his reverie.

'Sorry to drag you down here, Jack,' he said. 'I know you've got enough on your plate with Annabelle Roper but someone just put a window through.'

'So I heard. You got him, though, I think?'

'Yeah, he's being booked in now. Young fellow. However, it's not done much to calm things down. Thought you might want to say a few words. They'll listen to you after what you said at the council meeting this morning. They think you're on their side.'

'I made it clear that I do not do sides.'

'You try telling that to Miriam Canley,' said the uniformed inspector. 'She thinks you're her knight in shining armour.'

'I've been called many things but never that.' Harris gestured towards the two young men, who were still yelling profanities. 'Any idea who they are?'

'Nope, but it was their pal that we arrested for putting the window out. Lad called Jason Craig.'

'Craig, eh?' said Harris. 'His name has already cropped up once today.'

'I don't think they're from round here. The car they came in has a Newcastle registration and Craig gave an address in the city. We haven't had time to check if it's genuine but, if you ask me, someone has hijacked the protest.'

'I'm sure you're right. I'm not quite sure why, though. It doesn't make sense. It's a very local issue.'

'Clearly, someone does not agree.' The uniformed inspector gestured to the television crews filming the protestors. 'What's more, neither do they. It's gone national, apparently. Sky are having a field day.'

Harris noticed protest leader Miriam Canley standing nearby, watching the protest with a worried look on her face. He gestured for her to come and join him. As she walked over, one look at her uneasy expression was enough to confirm that things were not going the way she had planned.

'What the hell's happening, Miriam?' said Harris. 'I hardly think that smashing windows will do your cause much good, do you?'

'I didn't mean it to happen.' She seemed close to tears. 'This is meant to be a peaceful protest.'

'Tell that to the woman who was showered with glass,' said Harris. 'I don't imagine that she thinks it's peaceful. You really do need to tone things down, Miriam.'

'But I don't know the young man who did it.'

'Not sure that matters. Him and his pals are part of the protest and you're the organiser. If things get any worse, we're looking at all sorts of public order offences and you'd be one of the first people we'd arrest.' Harris looked at the uniformed inspector. 'Am I right?'

'Oh, aye,' said the inspector. 'I can't let this continue.'

'Don't you think it's time to call this off before someone gets hurt?' said Harris.

'I thought you were on our side, Jack.' She sounded disappointed.

'I keep telling you, Miriam, I don't do sides. My job is to uphold the law.'

'Yes, well, we have a right to have our voice heard.'

'And we have the right to lock you all up for breach of the peace. Time to end the protest.'

'Then the council will have won. James Hall will have got his way again, won't he? All this will have been for nothing.'

'That's democracy,' said Harris.

'Yes, but–'

'Look, Miriam, I have enough on my plate and the last thing I need is having to waste time on a bunch of middle-class do-gooders who should know better.'

Miriam looked hurt.

'Is that what you think we are?' she said.

Harris did not reply. Miriam looked as if she was about to remonstrate further but, as she did so, a stone flew from the ranks of the protestors towards the police line. It struck a female officer on the helmet and she cried out and recoiled, clutching her face. Blood spurted from a gash to her cheek.

'Look, Miriam,' said Harris with an urgency in his voice as fellow officers went to her assistance, 'I appreciate that feelings are running high with what happened to Annabelle but this is not the way to go about things. All this does is play into the hands of James Hall. He'll be loving this.'

'What do you mean?'

Harris gestured over to the television crews filming the protest.

'This is going out all over the country,' he said. 'Who knows, it may even be shown abroad and what will the viewers see? Protestors smashing windows and chucking stones at the police. All that does is allow James Hall to take the moral high ground. Much more of this and the folks at Rowan House will be seen as the innocent victims of mob mentality, and you'll never get the place closed down.'

Miriam considered the comment for a moment, frowned as another stone thudded into the police lines, then nodded.

'Alright,' she said.

She walked back to her fellow protestors. After an animated conversation lasting several minutes, it was clear that a grudging agreement had been reached and people slowly started to drift away, some of them shooting angry looks in the inspector's direction. He ignored them; Jack Harris had never really cared what people thought about him. The inspector saw the two young men turn towards their car and he walked over to intercept them.

'Gentlemen,' he said with a smile behind which lurked menace. 'Would you like to tell me what you are doing here?'

'We have every right—' began one of the men.

'I don't know what your game is,' said Harris in a voice so low that only they could hear, 'but if I ever see you in my fucking town again, I'll make damned sure they lock you up and throw away the key. We've already got your pal. I'm more than happy for you to join him.'

The other man opened his mouth to protest.

'Might I suggest that you consider your next words very carefully,' said Harris. 'Very carefully, indeed. They tell me that the food in our cells is particularly poor. Not that you'll care about that if you have to suck it up through a straw.'

The man looked at the glint in the detective's eye, scowled and brushed past the detective, followed by his friend.

'Good choice,' said Harris as they walked away. 'Mind how you go now.'

The men glared balefully at him but continued to walk away until they reached their vehicle. Harris watched with grim satisfaction as the car made its way down the leafy lane then turned the corner and vanished from sight. Ten minutes later, the road was almost deserted and the media and the police were packing up to go. A couple of reporters approached Harris, seeking an interview, but he waved them away.

'Talk to the press office,' he said.

The uniformed inspector walked over to Harris.

'Thanks, Jack,' he said.

'No bother. Your girl OK?'

'May need a couple of stitches but that's all,' said the uniformed inspector. 'What did you say to those lads?'

'You don't want to know,' said Harris.

'You're probably right,' said the inspector and gave a low laugh. 'I don't imagine that I'll find it in Philip Curtis's *Manual on Fostering Good Community Relations*.'

'I don't imagine you will.'

The uniformed inspector grinned, patted Harris on the shoulder and headed back to oversee the departure of his team. Harris noticed three women walking towards them. He recognised them as mothers from the town whose daughters attended Roxham Comprehensive.

'Chief Inspector,' said one of them. 'Can we have a word?'

'Surely. What can I do for you?'

'Is it true that Annabelle was forced to take MDMA?'

'It's likely, yes.'

'Do you know who did it?' she asked.

'Not yet,' said Harris. 'Why? Is there something you want to tell me?'

'Just that we're frightened that it could happen to our girls,' said one of the other women.

'In which case it would help if you could tell me what you know.'

'We don't know anything.' She looked at the others, who nodded. 'That's the problem, Chief Inspector. Just what we hear – that our children know where to get hold of drugs.'

'Do you know who is selling to them?' asked Harris. He lowered his voice. 'Just between you and me? No one will know that it was you that told me.'

The women shook their heads.

'They won't tell us,' said one of them.

'Well, if you hear anything, let me know.'

'Just keep our children safe,' she said.

'I'll do my best,' said Harris. He watched them walk back across the road. 'I just hope it's good enough.'

Harris noticed James Hall standing on the front step of Rowan House, watching proceedings with a concerned look on his face. The inspector walked up the drive.

'Your secretary OK?' asked Harris.

'A bit shaken but uninjured,' replied Hall. 'She's very lucky. A big shard of glass just missed her. Thank you for getting rid of them.'

'Saying that must have stuck in your craw.'

'Look, I have no desire to fall out with you, Chief Inspector,' said Hall. It sounded genuine; his tone of voice was less confrontational than it had been during their meeting earlier in the day. 'Besides, we're not that different.'

'And how do you work that out?'

'We may disagree on certain things but, at the end of the day, we're only doing our jobs and neither my staff nor your officers should have to put up with that kind of behaviour. Is your officer alright?'

'She'll live.'

Hall glanced at the shattered office window.

'I'll be demanding compensation, of course,' he said.

'I'm sure that the court will award it after we've charged the little toerag,' said Harris. 'Though quite what he and his mates were doing here, I'm not sure yet. You got any idea?'

Hall did not reply but something about his demeanour alerted the inspector's instincts.

'Is there something you want to tell me?' asked the detective. 'Do you know why Jason Craig and his pals turned up to the protest?'

'We live in an increasing angry world. People think they can do and say whatever they want. I blame Facebook.'

'That's a very glib answer,' said Harris. 'Why do I think there's more to it than that?'

The centre manager looked like he was going to elaborate on the comment but instead he turned back into the house.

'You have a very suspicious mind, Chief Inspector,' he said. 'Thanks, anyway.'

'Something tells me that you know more than you're letting on, Mr Hall.'

Hall turned and shook his head.

'You should know that I always find out people's little secrets in the end,' said Harris. 'I am sure that it won't take long for us to get it out of Jason Craig. If he's angry enough to risk arrest, he may be only too keen to tell us the reason. Even if he isn't, I can be very persuasive when I put my mind to it.'

Hall sighed.

'I imagine that you can,' he said. 'Come into my office. There's something you should see.'

'OK,' said Harris.

Once they were in the office, Hall opened a drawer in the filing cabinet, produced a sheaf of papers, which he handed to the detective without speaking, and took his seat behind his desk. Harris flicked through each of the pieces of paper; they were adorned with letters crudely cut out of newspaper headlines to form death threats.

'Delightful,' said the inspector.

'They've been arriving ever since it was announced that we had been shortlisted for the award.'

'And why did you not mention this before?' asked Harris. He placed the papers on the desk, sat back in his chair and looked at James Hall. 'No one should have to receive this kind of rubbish.'

'And what would you have done? Everyone knows the police would like to see us closed down.'

'That would not have affected our approach to the letters. As I keep telling people, we don't take sides.'

'Maybe,' said Hall. 'Anyway, we didn't want to inflame the situation.'

'We?'

'Gerald Gault has had three or four of them posted to County Hall. It's really shaken him up. He showed great courage in voting in our favour this morning.'

'Then why the hell did you not bring them to us?' Harris held up the papers; he could not conceal his exasperation. 'If you'd done that, we could have done something to stop–'

'The world is full of crackerjacks, Chief Inspector. We were worried that if it became public knowledge, it would only serve to encourage whoever was sending them. The oxygen of publicity and all that. These people thrive on it, you know. The person who sent the letters would love it.'

'Jason Craig, I am assuming?'

Hall looked surprised.

'It doesn't take Sherlock Holmes to work it out,' said Harris. 'He was the one who threw the brick through the window. Do you think he sent the death threats as well?'

'I imagine so, yes. I am pretty sure that he is also going by the name of Ricky B on Facebook. He's been posting some pretty inflammatory things about me and Rowan House.'

'So my sergeant tells me.'

'I was rather hoping that he was one of those people who sit in front of the computer in their underpants, not the type to actually do anything about it.' Hall sighed. 'Then he turned up at County Hall this morning. That's when I knew he was serious.'

'You know what he looks like then?'

'We've met before, unfortunately.'

'So, why has he got it in for you?' asked the inspector.

'I am afraid that the story does not exactly reflect well on me. Or on Rowan House, for that matter. If it ever got out, it could cause incalculable damage to the reputation of—'

'Hang your bloody reputation!' exclaimed Harris. 'If something is happening in my area, I need to know. I've got two dead teenagers on my hands, a bunch of troublemakers hurling stones at your centre and a PC on her way to hospital to have a hole in her face stitched up. I am not really interested in protecting reputations.'

Hall nodded gloomily.

'No,' he said, 'I don't suppose you are. It was a couple of years ago. I was running a similar centre to this in Newcastle. It's where Gerald Gault got the idea for Rowan House. It's why he approached me to set it up. He had heard about the work we were doing.'

'And the link with Jason Craig?'

'One of the young men referred to us in Newcastle was a lad called Andy Craig. Jason's kid brother. He'd just turned fifteen. He was running wild and the juvenile court wanted us to try to put him straight.'

'And did you?'

'No.' Hall shook his head sadly. 'We tried everything, we really did, but he never settled. It just wasn't for him. We never claim to have a hundred percent success rate with our boys.'

'Not something I heard you admit in the council meeting.'

'The councillors were jittery enough,' said Hall. 'The last thing I wanted to do was put more doubts in their mind. You saw how tight the vote was. Something like this could have tipped it the other way.'

'Why was Andy before the juvenile court?'

'Dealing drugs at his school.'

'Drugs?' said Harris. 'What kind of drugs?'

'Cannabis mainly. Some heroin.'

'So what happened to him?'

Hall hesitated.

'It would only take my sergeant one click of a mouse to find out,' said Harris. 'It'll be on record somewhere.'

'I suppose it was going to come out anyway,' said Hall with another sigh. 'I expelled Andy. I don't do things like that without serious consideration but he was not buying into what we were trying to do. He ended up in a juvenile detention centre where someone smuggled in heroin and he took an overdose. The staff found his body in the toilets one lunchtime.'

Hall turned heavy eyes on the inspector; they were glistening with tears.

'It's why I am so protective of our boys,' he said. 'They're so vulnerable.'

Harris looked at him for a few moments and, briefly, only briefly, felt the faintest stirrings of sympathy. But then he thought of the grief-stricken families of Ellie Cross and Annabelle Roper and of the distressed victims trying to come to terms with Lee Smedley's burglaries. Of their tears, of the sleepless nights lying staring at the ceiling and straining to hear every sound in the darkness for fear that it was another intruder. *Whose side are you on, Jack?* Harris felt his attitude hardening again. He didn't like the idea that anyone should even think it was a question they could ask of him.

'Vulnerable, they may be,' said the inspector. 'But they have to be held to account for their actions. I am assuming that Jason blames you for what happened to his brother?'

'He does, yes. That's how I guessed that he was Ricky B, from some of the things he was saying on Facebook. He never mentioned his brother by name – I suppose he wanted to protect his identity in case we did report the letters to the police – but it was pretty clear what he was talking about. I tell you, he's on a crusade.'

'That's twice that word has cropped up today,' said Harris. 'Exactly what kind of crusade do you think he's on?'

'I hate to think.'

'Yeah,' he murmured, 'so do I.'

Chapter ten

Lee Smedley lounged on the threadbare sofa, took a swig from a can of strong, cheap lager and looked across at Rad, who was sitting on a rickety armchair.

'So, what do we do now?' asked Smedley. 'You want to risk another run to Levton Bridge?'

They were sitting in the living room of a council house on one of Newcastle's sprawling housing estates. The air was damp and musty and scattered around them was the detritus of dissolute lives, empty pizza boxes which had been there for days, half-eaten Chinese takeaway meals in crumpled containers and the paraphernalia of drug-taking: needles, tin foil, cigarette papers. A television in the corner of the room was showing a Sky News report about the protest outside Rowan House.

'Not yet,' said Rad.

He took a draw on a hand-rolled cigarette and watched as a photograph of an attractive blonde girl in school uniform flashed onto the screen. *Murdered schoolgirl Annabelle Roper*, said the caption.

'Are you sure you ain't involved with what happened to that girl?' said Rad. 'The report earlier said she was going out with someone from Rowan House. Was that you?'

'In her dreams.'

Rad looked unconvinced.

'Is that why you're here?' asked Rad. 'Are the cops looking for you?'

'Relax.' Smedley took another swig of lager. 'I'm in the clear. She wasn't my girlfriend and there's no way anyone will tell the cops otherwise. I got things wrapped up nice and tight in Levton Bridge, I have. There's no way anyone is going to grass me up.'

Still, Rad looked sceptical. He was used to dealing with criminals but there had always been something different about Lee Smedley, a sense of animal cunning which was unnerving in one so young. Rad had often wondered what would happen if Smedley turned on him, if he refused to take orders and tried instead to seize the initiative. The others had already warned him that Smedley was not to be trusted, that Rad should sever their ties. His arrival in Newcastle was unwelcome, particularly as Rad was picking up rumours that the police had been stepping up their activities against drug dealers in the city. Some DCI had been tasked with tracking down dealers. Maybe, thought Rad as he watched events unfold on the television screen, today was the day to find out if his friend's concerns about the teenager were well-founded.

Smedley noticed his uneasy expression.

'Don't worry,' he said.

The teenager drained the can and tossed it onto the floor where it nestled alongside several more. He reached down the side of the chair and produced another one, which he snapped open.

'I ain't got nowt to do with Annabelle Roper's death,' he said. 'Or that other girl last month, neither. They took MDMA.'

'Yes, but…'

'I'm in the clear, Rad, and you're in the clear as well. I'm dead careful, me.'

'You better be sure about that, Lee. I don't want this fucking up.'

'I am sure, man.' Smedley took a gulp of lager and wiped his mouth with the back of his hand. 'So, when *are* we going to do another run then? We got plenty of customers at the school. They're just waiting for me to bring the gear in and I reckon I can sell as much stuff as you–'

'It's too risky with everything that's going on.'

'But I want my money.'

Rad decided that it was time to reassert control.

'You'll be lucky if that's all you get if you turn out to be lying about them kids,' he said. 'The cops will be after you for murder. We're not doing another run just yet and that's final.'

He tried to look unconcerned as Smedley considered the comment. Rad heaved a secret sigh of relief when the teenager nodded.

'OK,' said Smedley. 'You're the boss.'

'I am.' Rad reached into his trouser pocket and produced a roll of ten pound notes. He peeled several off and held them out. 'In the meantime, there's fifty quid, that should keep you going.'

Smedley took the money.

'Thanks,' he said.

Rad turned his attention back to the television as the news report showed footage of a protesting Jason Craig being hauled away by police officers after throwing the brick through the Rowan House window. Rad looked thoughtfully at the screen.

'I know him,' he said. 'The twat went for me with a broken bottle in a pub one night. Reckoned I'd sold the drugs that killed his kid brother.'

'And had you?'

'Fuck knows,' said Rad. 'Do you know him?'

Smedley looked at the television and shook his head.

'Na,' he said. 'Never seen him before.'

'So, you've got no idea what he was doing in Levton Bridge then?'

'Maybe he's got summat against Rowan House,' said Smedley. 'The folks up there are going fucking bonkers about the place and there was some meeting about it this morning. Council or something. The bloke who runs Rowan House reckons people were going to try to close it down.'

'And did they succeed?'

Smedley shrugged.

'What do I care?' he said.

'Because you live there.'

'Only because I was sent there. I can leave whenever I want.'

'Well, I don't like it.' Rad took a drag on his cigarette. 'There's far too much attention on the place. Too many journalists. Best to wait for this little lot to die down before we send you back with any gear, I reckon. Maybe give it two or three weeks, yeah?'

Smedley looked for a moment as if he was about to protest but thought better of it and took another swig of lager.

'You call the shots,' he said.

Only this time it didn't seem to Rad that he meant it.

Chapter eleven

'You've been holding out on us, Councillor,' said Jack Harris. 'And I don't like people who do that.'

Sitting behind his desk at County Hall in Roxham, planning committee chairman Gerald Gault nervously surveyed the grim-faced inspector and the equally stern Matty Gallagher as they took their seats opposite him. The politician was worried; the memories of his disagreement with the inspector at that morning's meeting were still fresh in his mind and he'd heard what people said about the way the detective reacted when he was crossed.

'I don't know what you mean,' he said.

'Oh, but I think you do.' Harris opened the brown envelope that he had placed on the desk. He slid out photocopies of the death threats sent to James Hall. 'Care for a game of Snap, Mr Chairman?'

Gault looked sick.

'Where did you get those?' he said.

'James Hall,' said Harris. 'He tried to keep them from us as well but, like I told him and like I'll tell you now, there's no such thing as a secret in our world.'

Gault sighed, reached into a drawer and produced his own threatening letters, which he placed with exaggerated care next to the photocopies, taking several seconds to ensure that they were straight.

'In a way, I'm glad it's all in the open,' he said. 'I haven't been able to sleep.'

'Then why keep them from us?' asked Gallagher. 'We could have helped you.'

'I had rather hoped that they would stop.'

'But they didn't, did they?' said the sergeant. He tapped the top photocopy with a forefinger. 'These people tend to keep going unless someone catches them.'

'I imagine they do,' said Gault bleakly. 'The latest one arrived this morning. Just before the council meeting.'

'You really should have come to us,' said Harris.

'And what good would that have done?' Gault could contain his dissatisfaction no longer. 'Everyone knows that the police want to see Rowan House closed. They all heard what you said this morning. Everyone knows whose side you're on.'

'We don't take sides,' said Harris. 'I keep telling people that and I resent the suggestion that we would have ignored you. In fact, I'm sick of people telling me what I would or would not have done.'

'Yes, but—'

'If we'd known about these threats, we could have found out who was sending them. Although I think that you already know that, do you not? The same person who has been hassling you on Facebook. Our friend Ricky B.'

Gault nodded glumly.

'I take it you know why he's doing it?' asked Harris.

'James told me.'

'Well, you can stop worrying now. We've got him in custody up at Levton Bridge. He chucked a brick through a window at Rowan House.'

'That was him, was it? Can't say I'm surprised. What will happen to him?'

'He'll be charged with criminal damage,' said Harris. 'And if you agree to help us, we might be able to get him for threatening behaviour as well. Will you give us a statement?'

'I would rather let things lie.'

'I still don't understand why you didn't think you could trust us. The force does an immense amount of work with the council, does it not? Matty here has been working with you on that campaign to educate old people about cold calling and another one of our officers has been training your social workers how to spot–'

'My reluctance to give you a statement is nothing to do with the police,' said Gault. He looked unhappily at the officers. 'The truth isn't very palatable, I am afraid.'

'It rarely is,' said Harris. 'Are you protecting someone?'

'I am protecting myself, Chief Inspector. I am afraid it's a case of good old-fashioned hubris. A fear of what it might do to my reputation if all this becomes public knowledge.'

Harris snorted.

'I've heard just about enough about reputation today,' he said.

'I would not expect you to understand.'

'I understand self-serving politicians well enough.'

'That's unfair.' Gault leaned forward. There was a fire in his eyes and his voice quivered with emotion. 'I have invested a lot in Rowan House, Chief Inspector. Politically, I mean. I had to fight hard to persuade my fellow councillors to approve the project in the first place, then even harder to persuade them to make it permanent after all the trouble. My reputation was on the line this morning. Can you imagine what they would have said if they knew about the death threats? Some of them were wavering, as it was. And if the award panel gets to hear about it, there's every chance that they would withdraw–'

'There's more important things than awards.'

'James said that you would say something like that. That's why we were reluctant to come to you. I know that you dislike Rowan House and–'

'I dislike it because some of the boys are responsible for the increase in crime in my area and now there's every reason to believe that one of them is involved in the murder of young Annabelle Roper. And who knows, perhaps with the death of Ellie Cross? Kids like that need protecting, not Lee Smedley and his cronies.'

It was Harris's turn to show strong feelings and he was talking rapidly now.

'You want to know about unpalatable truths, Councillor?' he said. 'Do you? My unpalatable truth is that I am terrified that I'll have more dead kids on my hands unless we can stop the drugs coming in. That there are more Annabelles and Ellies out there. The thought makes me sick to the stomach so you'll forgive me if I don't get too bent out of shape about your fucking award.'

Gault looked shocked at the profanity and Gallagher watched his boss with surprise; he had never seen Jack Harris lose control of his inner emotions. His temper, yes, all the time, but his inner emotions, no.

'I think what DCI Harris is saying,' said the sergeant as Harris paused for breath, leaning forward and tapping the photocopies again, 'is that you'd better make that statement. Don't you think?'

The politician reached into his desk for a piece of paper and a pen; something told him that it wasn't really a question from the sergeant. Harris watched him begin to write and nodded his approval. The inspector was back in control of his emotions.

Half an hour later, as it started to rain, the detectives were back in Harris's Land Rover, heading up the winding road out of Roxham in the direction of Levton Bridge, the councillor's statement in the envelope nestling in the passenger seat footwell. They travelled in silence for a few minutes, Gallagher staring out of the window, alone with his thoughts, Harris staring straight ahead as he drove them. As the road started to climb and farmers' fields gave way to the beginnings of bleak moorland, Gallagher glanced across at his boss.

'You OK?' he said.

'Yeah, why?'

'Well, your outburst back there...'

'It was nothing.'

'It didn't sound like nothing.'

'It was honestly felt, Matty lad,' said the inspector. 'You know as well as I do that there have been plenty of deaths of young people in small country towns down to drugs and that they tend to come in spates. I am worried that the same thing could happen here. Ellie Cross becomes Annabelle Roper becomes some other kid, becomes half a dozen...'

'I know what you mean.' Gallagher sensed that there was more to come from his boss. 'That's all that's bugging you then?'

'Isn't it enough?'

'It's just that you've been a bit off over the past few days. A bit distracted.'

Harris slowed the vehicle and steered left to allow a tractor through. Manoeuvre completed, he glanced across at the sergeant and sighed.

'You're not going to let this drop, are you?' he said.

'I will if it's something that you don't want to talk about. It would just be nice to know. If it's something that has an effect on our operations.'

'Fair comment,' said Harris.

The inspector hesitated for a few moments. Tried to find the right words. His mind drifted back again to the bodies in the forest clearing but he did not want to confide to the sergeant that he was experiencing flashbacks. That the counsellor's warnings all those years ago were finally coming true. That the phone call had triggered something deep inside him. That he was worried about what was happening to him. He hadn't told anyone, not even his girlfriend, and he did not feel ready to break his silence.

Not yet. Maybe not ever. The inspector realised that Gallagher was staring at him. That he was expecting him to say something.

'Are you sure you're alright?' asked the sergeant.

'Yeah, I am. Nothing to worry about, Matty lad. It's just that I rang Jenny last night and she said something that made me think.'

'Jesus, you not thinking of having kids, are you?' exclaimed the sergeant.

Gallagher was genuinely taken aback. The inspector had been in a relationship with Jenny Armannsson, head of the fraud squad at Greater Manchester Police, for the best part of a year after they met on a joint investigation between the forces. However, no one at Levton Bridge knew how serious their liaison was. This was a major revelation from the normally secretive inspector.

'I didn't think that it had gone that far between the two of you,' said the sergeant.

'No, no, it hasn't. We're taking it steady but you have to think about these things, don't you? I mean, don't tell me that you and Julie haven't discussed having kids?'

'Yeah, of course we have. Loads of times but we've been together for fifteen years. I mean... you and kids... it's...'

Gallagher's voice tailed off as it was his turn to struggle to find the right words; he and Harris may have worked closely for several years but, away from the job, it had never been a close relationship. Harris had always been a loner and the sergeant had only visited the inspector's cottage on a hillside outside Levton Bridge a couple of times. Normally, Harris retreated there alone when he finished work, him, his dogs, his whisky bottle and his wildlife books. And as for the inspector's love life, no one had seen Harris and Armannsson out together. Rumour had it that they met away from the prying eyes of a community where everyone knew your business.

'Hey,' said Harris, noting the sergeant's continuing silence, 'you better not be thinking about spreading gossip all over the station. I'm just telling you because, like you say, you need to know.'

'No, of course I won't. I'm just...' Gallagher gave up when once more he could not find the words. 'So, what exactly did she say?'

'Had I ever thought about having kids.'

'Was she suggesting it?'

'Don't know.'

'And have you thought about having kids?'

'No. I'm far too selfish for that.'

'Get away.'

Harris let the comment go.

'However, it did get me thinking.' He guided the vehicle round a tight bend and the road started to climb more steeply. 'I mean, it *could* happen one day, couldn't it? Then this morning, there I was looking down at the body of Annabelle Roper. She had it all ahead of her before Lee Smedley took it away from her.'

'You still reckon it could be down to him then?'

'Why would he leg it if it's not? And Alistair says that his mate got all shifty when he started asking questions.'

'Danny Cairns is always shifty,' said the sergeant. 'They're as bad as each other.'

'But Danny didn't run, did he?'

'I guess not.'

Silence settled on the vehicle again as the first spots of rain soon turned into a downpour and the wind started to blow harder across the hills. Gallagher stared gloomily out at the darkening moors. As a Londoner born and bred, he had never come to terms with the sudden changes of weather that characterised the North Pennines. A thought struck him and he looked across at Harris.

'Jesus,' he said. 'What if it's a boy? Another Jack Harris? The world really is not ready for that.'

'Could be a Jaqueline. Have you thought of that?'

'Fucking hell. That might be even worse.'

'No respect,' said Harris but he was smiling. 'That's your problem, Matty lad. Besides, I told you, we're not thinking of having kids so you can forget that for a start. However, it does make you think about the kind of world we bring our young people into.'

'A wonderful one full of opportunity. For the vast majority of them, anyway.'

'Yes, but not for all of them, though. Not for Annabelle Roper or Ellie Cross. Jenny also reminded me that children change everything, that officers who are normally level-headed can lose their sense of perspective when there's kids involved – even the best of them. We have to be careful on this one.'

'You thinking of anyone in particular?' asked the sergeant. 'Something happened?'

'No. It's just something to bear in mind, though. Jenny told me about one of her first cases in CID – a guy who murdered a fourteen-year-old girl. The investigation was led by a DCI, as solid and reliable as they came, but he lost it when he was interviewing the suspect. The guy smirked and the DCI punched him and ended up being kicked out of the force. GMP damn near lost the conviction.'

'It happens.'

'Yes, well, we have to guard against it happening here. Curtis said the same thing.' Harris hesitated. 'I reckon he might have been referring to me.'

'I'm sure he wasn't. I know you have a temper on you but there's no way that you would push it that far.'

'You sure about that?' said Harris. 'See, when I was listening to James Hall and Gerald Gault banging on about their precious reputations with hardly a thought for the girls, all I could think of was the body of Annabelle Roper.' He'd thought of the clearing as well but he was not about to tell the sergeant. 'I could cheerfully have throttled them.'

'We all feel like that from time to time,' said Gallagher. 'Besides, you kept it all under control, didn't you?'

'This time.'

They completed the remainder of the journey without speaking further, both men preoccupied with their own thoughts. For the sergeant's part, having been afforded a rare glimpse into the inspector's inner world, he could not shake the feeling that there was something he was not being told. The idea troubled him. Troubled him greatly.

Chapter twelve

The bell signalling the end of the school day at Roxham Comprehensive rang at 3:20pm and, with a sigh of relief, Alistair Marshall gathered up his papers and left the room. He was walking across the reception area when Angie Coulson gestured at him and pushed her way through the throng of pupils.

'Have you got a minute?' she asked.

'Sure.' He tried to sound professional. Like nothing had happened between them.

She led him into an empty office.

'What is it?' he asked. 'Have you heard something?'

She looked uncomfortable.

'I wanted to apologise,' she said. 'For what happened earlier. I was sharp with you and that was wrong.'

'You have nothing to apologise for, Angie. Everyone's on edge, I think. Besides, you were right, I was out of order. Shouldn't have asked you out. Not now anyway. Not exactly professional.'

'No, it was me who was out of order.' She gave a sad smile. 'The deaths... everyone's acting a bit strange, you know...'

'I understand.'

She reached out to gently touch his arm.

'Maybe we *can* have that drink,' she said. 'I mean, we're adults, aren't we? I'm sure we know how to behave. But not tonight, though. I don't think I could stomach it tonight. The kids mean the world to me and I'm finding it difficult to come to terms with what's happened.'

Marshall reached up to touch her hand.

'I understand,' he said. 'Let me know when you're ready. You've got my number.'

She nodded and left the room. Marshall stood on his own for a few moments then punched the air.

'Result,' he said eventually. 'Reeesult!'

A couple of minutes later, he was walking through the mass of boisterous young people who were jostling along the main drive leading away from the building. The wary looks from some of the students were not lost on the detective; they served only to strengthen his suspicions that some of the young people knew more than they were letting on. He had just reached the car park when he saw a familiar figure standing on the main road, not far from the gates, a slim girl with tousled blonde hair, wearing jeans and a blue T-shirt. He recognised her immediately as Tracey Malham.

'Gotcha,' he murmured.

The detective edged his vehicle out of the car park and out onto the road where, having realised that she had been spotted, Tracey was walking briskly away from the school. Marshall swore as he was forced to wait for a couple of minutes to allow a large group of pupils to cross in front of him and by the time he caught up with Tracey she was well down the road. Marshall pulled up beside her, cut the engine and got out of the vehicle.

'Tracey,' he said. 'I've been looking for you.'

'I had a dentist's appointment.' She had stopped walking and turned towards him but her sullen demeanour made it clear that she had no desire to talk to him.

'Try again.' He gave her a stern look but she did not reply. 'We can continue this down the police station, if you would prefer.'

'Why did you want to talk to me anyway?' She gave him a look of defiance. 'I ain't done nothing wrong. I told Miss Coulson that.'

'Then how come you did a runner when you heard I was looking for you?' He gestured to her clothes. 'Truancy is a very serious offence, you know, Tracey. Could land you in court. And your parents, for that matter. They could end up before the magistrates. And in the local newspaper.'

'No one reads newspapers anymore.'

'On their website then. Not sure your mum and dad will fancy their names splashed all over that, do you?'

'Why are you interested in no-shows anyway?' she said. 'You not got nothing better to do?'

'Actually. I have. How about investigating a murder, for starters?'

'What do you mean?' said Tracey. She seemed less confident now. More guarded. 'I told Miss Coulson that I don't know owt about what happened to Annabelle last night. And I don't know who gave her that MDMA.'

'And how do you know that she died from taking MDMA?'

'Everyone knows.'

'You can see why we are interested in you, can't you? You *were* with her the last time she went missing.'

'So?' Her belligerence was back. 'We was only smoking cannabis. I don't know nothing about no MDMA. Too dangerous.'

'Nevertheless, I still want to know if you were with Annabelle last night. See, I don't trust you, Tracey. I'm not sure I trust any of you.'

'Think what you want. I ain't telling you nowt. You'll only fit us up.'

'Fit you up for what?' asked Marshall.

'I ain't saying.'

She started walking away and Marshall reached out and grabbed her arm, twisting her round to face him.

'Hey!' she exclaimed. 'You're hurting us! Let go!'

'Not until you tell me the truth.'

'That's abuse, that is.' She wriggled her arm free and glanced along the road; the nearest group of pupils was a hundred metres away. 'I know my rights. There ain't no witnesses, neither. Just my word against yours. I'll get you sacked!'

Marshall let go and held up his hands in surrender.

'OK, OK,' he said. 'But I'm serious, Tracey, if you don't talk to me, I *will* arrest you.'

'For what?' She stared at him, defying the constable to try. 'I didn't kill Annabelle and you've got nowt to say I did.'

'I can still arrest you for obstructing a murder inquiry.' Marshall gave her a hard look to emphasise the point. 'Fancy a night in the cells, do you?'

Noting her resolve wavering, he softened his voice.

'Look, Tracey,' he said, 'I don't want to get heavy about this, I really don't. I just want to know what happened to Annabelle. We all do.'

Tracey considered the comment.

'I guess you were fair enough with me last time,' she said. 'You could have thrown the book at us. If I tell you something, will you leave me alone?'

'Depends what you say.'

Tracey noticed a group of schoolgirls walking down the road towards them, giggling and shouting.

'OK,' she said. 'I'll help you but only because my dad will bray us if I get nicked again.'

'Fair enough.'

'Down here.' She pointed down an alleyway running between a couple of houses. 'I don't want no one to see me talking to you.'

'As long as you don't pull the abuse stunt again.'

'I won't.' Tracey gave a slight smile. 'Besides, you ain't my type.'

Marshall followed her down the alleyway. When she was sure that they were far enough away not to be overheard, Tracey turned to face him.

'OK, yeah,' she said. 'I *was* with Annabelle last night but she was alive when I left her.'

'What were you doing?'

'Smoking weed. Like last time.'

'Where? Behind the bandstand in the park again?'

'Na. We were near the tyre place on Ronaldsway Road. There's a bit of wasteland. No one can see you.'

'I know it,' said Marshall. 'When was this?'

'We met up about six-thirty but I left at eight-thirty.'

'How come you're so sure about the time?' he asked.

'My dad says I have to be home for nine. After what happened to Ellie, you know. He goes spare if I'm late.'

'What condition was Annabelle in when you left her?' asked Marshall. 'Stoned?'

'She weren't that bad, no. Neither of us was but I ain't got no idea what happened to her after that.' Shouts at the far end of the alleyway caught her attention and she stared anxiously towards the road. She relaxed when a group of girls passed by without noticing them. When she looked back at the detective, he saw that her eyes were moist.

'I could have saved her,' she said. She was fighting back tears now. 'I mean, made sure that she got home safe. She didn't deserve to die. Not like that. No one does.'

'Which is why we want to find out what happened. Like how come she ended up next to Rowan House and who gave her the MDMA? Who else was with you last night?'

Tracey hesitated.

'I can still arrest you,' said Marshall.

'I can't tell you.'

'Please,' said Marshall. His voice was soft again. 'We really do need to know what happened, Tracey. Two teenagers have died already, two of your fellow pupils, and we have to find out what's happening before there's a third – you, maybe. Who knows, depending on how helpful you are, I may even be able to keep your name out of it?'

She considered the comment and nodded.

'You had better be straight up, mind,' she said. 'You can't tell no one it came from me.'

'OK?'

'We were with Lee.'

'Lee Smedley?' said Marshall. 'So, they *were* going out?'

'I don't think it was a boyfriend-girlfriend thing. Annabelle made all the running but he knocks around with a lot of girls from the school, does Lee. I don't think she were anything special to him.'

'Anyone else there last night?'

'Danny Cairns,' she said. 'But that's all I dare say. You don't want to get on the wrong side of them, especially not Lee.'

'Why?'

'You work it out.'

'Are you saying they killed her?'

'I don't know who killed her. And don't ask me about Danny, neither. I hardly know him. He was Annabelle's friend, really.'

Marshall looked at her for a few moments, trying to rationalise what he was being told. She seemed genuine, uneasy. Scared, even. He reached out and touched her gently on the shoulder.

'Thank you,' he said. 'It's enough.'

This time, she did not protest at his touch.

* * *

Jack Harris and his dogs had just returned to his office when the desk phone rang. The inspector reached over and picked up the receiver.

'Hi, it's Mel,' said a woman's voice. 'Have you interviewed Jason Craig yet?'

'I'm just about to.' He sat down behind his desk. The animals lapped greedily from the water bowls in the corner of the room. 'Why, have you got something interesting for me?'

'Could well have. I take it that it's too much to ask if you have checked your emails recently?'

'Not if I can avoid it,' said Harris. 'Why?'

'Because I've just sent you a couple of documents that might be of interest. You know I said that the name Jason Craig rang a bell but I couldn't quite remember why? Well, it turns out that uniform lifted him a year ago.'

'For what?'

'You'll see,' said Garside. 'Oh, and be warned when you interview him – our Mr Craig would appear to have a bit of a temper on him.'

'Tell me about it. He chucked a brick through a window at Rowan House. Nearly put some secretary's eye out.'

'That's just the half of it,' said Mel Garside. 'If you ask me, Jason Craig is lucky that he's not inside.'

Chapter thirteen

'So, Jason,' said Harris as he stared across the interview room desk at the young man, 'the big question is how do you fit into today's events? We would love to know, wouldn't we, DI Roberts?'

The dark-haired woman sitting next to him nodded. Gillian Roberts was Levton Bridge's only detective inspector, the organiser whose carefully cultivated matronly demeanour masked a mind as sharp as they came. As the mother of two teenage boys, both of whom attended Roxham Comprehensive, she had viewed the recent deaths with growing alarm, not least because one of her sons had admitted to smoking cannabis. She lived in fear that he'd go onto something harder. Like all the town's parents, she had heard the rumours about the drugs in circulation and, as ever in such cases, had found herself torn between her responsibilities as a mother and her duty as a police officer. However hard she pressed her boys, though, they professed to knowing nothing about MDMA. Roberts was not sure if they were telling the truth. The thought disturbed her. If she couldn't trust her own kids...

Now, she noted Jason Craig's resolute expression and sighed; it was the demeanour of yet another person who was not going to talk, so the detective inspector switched her attention to the duty solicitor, a slim woman in her thirties. Roberts knew Mari Jameson from their professional lives but also through the school; she'd seen her at parents' evenings because the lawyer was another mother with teenagers at Roxham Comprehensive. Now, sitting in the stuffy little interview room at Levton Bridge Police Station, the mother in Gillian Roberts shared the solicitor's concerns; the police officer wondered how best she could use the connection.

'Come on, Jason,' said Harris. 'The time for games is over. Are you going to tell me why you travelled all the way from Newcastle to chuck a brick through the window of Rowan House?'

'No.'

'It would certainly help if you did, lovey,' said Roberts. She tried to sound sympathetic and gave him a reassuring smile. The good cop, bad cop routine. 'You are in a lot of trouble, as things stand.'

'Where are my mates?' asked Craig.

'Still running, if they've got any sense,' said Harris.

Roberts gave a half-smile; everyone in the station had heard how Harris had collared them near Rowan House for one of his 'little chats'. The detective inspector had always struggled with some of the DCI's methods but she had to admit that they were usually effective.

Craig looked worried.

'Then how am I going to get home when I get released?' he asked.

'Who says you're going to be released?' said Harris. 'Like the DI says, son, you're in a lot of trouble.'

'I ain't saying nothing.'

'Miss Jameson,' said Roberts, glancing at the lawyer, 'it really would be best if your client co-operated. Emotions are running pretty high out there following Annabelle's death and your client is right in the middle of it. We need to understand why.'

'I would have to agree,' said the solicitor, thinking of her children. She looked at Craig. 'Jason, might I suggest that you–'

'I don't need to say anything,' said Craig. 'I know my rights and they can't keep me here just for smashing a window. They can't keep me in for that.'

'It's more than that, though,' said Harris. 'As Ricky B, you have been fomenting plenty of trouble in this town. I'm pretty sure that there's something in there that we can charge you with. Incitement, maybe. Enough to ask the court to remand you in custody for a few days anyway. Let us make further enquiries.'

'Yeah, well I'm still not going to say anything.'

'Fair enough,' said Harris. For a few moments he seemed to be engrossed by the contents of the print-out lying on the desk. Craig watched him with concern.

'What's that?' he asked.

'That? Oh, just something from Northumbria Police. Andy a bit of a druggie, was he? Overdose, wasn't it?'

Craig startled them as he leapt to his feet.

'You keep my brother out of this!' he shouted.

'Sit down,' said Harris.

The chief inspector noted the way Craig's right fist was bunching and un-bunching and that a vein was pulsing in his neck. Harris allowed himself a slight smile of satisfaction; you just had to know which buttons to press with people. The inspector noticed Gillian Roberts frown. He knew what she was thinking but, *stuff empathy*, he thought; he didn't have time to waste on niceties.

Craig remained standing, pointing a finger at the detective.

'I said sit down,' repeated Harris.

Mari Jameson placed a restraining hand on her client's arm and, after a few moments, he nodded and retook his seat.

'That was a cheap trick,' said Craig. Although he had regained his composure as rapidly as he had lost control of it, his voice was laden with resentment. 'A really cheap trick.'

'Not so cheap,' said the inspector. 'After all, your brother is why you came over here with your pals, isn't he? He is why you've been saying all those things on Facebook? To get back at James Hall. The man you blame for Andy's death. That's what this is all about, isn't it?'

'James Hall had it coming.' Craig spat the words out. 'He's a sanctimonious bastard.'

'Maybe he is, Jason, but he didn't force your brother to take the drugs, did he? Andy had a choice, unlike Annabelle Roper. Someone made her take MDMA last night and it killed her. That's murder.'

'Don't try and pin that on me,' said Craig. 'I don't know anything about that. All I'm interested in is James Hall.'

'I'm prepared to believe that,' said Harris. 'And I can see why. He's got a lot of questions to answer. In fact, since you are so vehemently and commendably anti-drugs, I was rather wondering if you wanted to help us? The last thing I want is another dead teenager on my hands.'

Craig looked at him suspiciously.

'Is this some kind of trick?' he asked.

'No trick, son. Co-operating with us has got to be better than throwing bricks through windows, hasn't it? Who knows, it might even allow you to get back at James Hall. That's what you want, isn't it?'

Craig gave the inspector a guarded look; the interview was not going the way he had expected but the opportunity to strike a blow against the manager of Rowan House intrigued him. He knew that the inspector was playing him but it was a temptation that he was struggling to resist. He glanced at his lawyer, confused, seeking guidance, less sure of himself.

'The least you can do is hear him out,' she said. 'Although I do have to say that your approach is somewhat unconventional, Chief Inspector. In different circumstances, I might even have been tempted to report your comments about a fellow professional to your commander but those girls…' Her voice tailed off as she thought of her daughter. 'You are right, we have to make sure that it does not happen again.'

'Agreed,' said Harris. 'Well, Jason, what's it to be? You going to tell us what you know about James Hall?'

'You think he's got something to do with the death of those girls?'

'That's what we want to know,' said Harris. He leaned forward and lowered his voice in conspiratorial fashion in an attempt to gain Craig's trust. 'Not to be repeated outside these four walls, there is a strong possibility that at least one of the boys from Rowan House is linked to the death of Annabelle. If there *is* a connection with Rowan House, it's in both our interests to prove it, is it not?'

'What would I have to do?'

'You can start by giving me the name of the person who is bringing drugs into Levton Bridge. We think it might be coming from Newcastle.'

Craig thought for a few moments then nodded.

'You're right about Rowan House,' he said. 'There's rumours that one of the boys goes over to Newcastle every two or three weeks to pick the stuff up.'

'What stuff?'

'I don't know exactly. Definitely cannabis.'

'And his name?'

'I just know it's a boy from Rowan House.'

'Come on, Jason.'

'Honest, I don't know his name.'

'OK. Do you know the supplier? The guy in Newcastle?'

'No.'

'You'll have to do better than that, if I am going to help you.' Harris picked up a second piece of paper from the desk. 'Tell me about Martin Radcliffe. Rad to his friends, I believe.'

'Never heard of him.'

'Really?' Harris scanned the charge sheet that had been emailed to him by Mel Garside. 'But surely you went for him with a broken bottle in a pub in Newcastle city centre last year. Accused him of selling your brother the drugs that killed him.'

'Ok, so I know him. What of it?'

'We are wondering if Rad also supplied the drugs that killed our teenagers. If you tell us what you know, it might help you get even.'

'I don't need you. I can sort it myself.'

'Not sure a three-month suspended sentence is the best way to do it,' said Harris. He glanced down at the charge sheet. 'According to the police in Newcastle, you were lucky not to go away for it. Now that you've been arrested here, you probably will. The court is likely to take a dim view of what's been happening, particularly when we charge you with sending death threats to James Hall and Councillor Gault.'

'You can't pin that on me.'

'You just try me. Come on, Jason, why not help us?'

'Why should I? The cops in Newcastle were more interested in getting me in court than what happened to Andy. They didn't want to know.'

'Well, I do. And I might be persuaded to turn a blind eye to your activities here. The Facebook posts and the broken window. Even the death threats. Play nicely with us and it all goes away.'

Craig glanced at his solicitor.

'Up to you, Jason,' she said. 'But it sounds like a good deal to me.'

'Look, lovey,' said Gillian Roberts, giving him a reassuring smile, 'no one should have to go through what your brother went through. You don't want another family to experience that, do you?'

Craig thought for a few moments.

'There's a house,' he said. Something about the DI's demeanour reminded him of his mother. Craig recalled her tears when the police officer stood in her living room and told her that her son had died. He recalled the tears she had shed every day since. 'On one of the housing estates in Newcastle. That's where Rad sells his drugs from.'

Harris slid a blank piece of paper across the table and handed Craig a pen.

'Just write it all down,' he said. 'Everything you know.'

Thirty minutes later, a satisfied Jack Harris and a troubled Gillian Roberts were on their way along the corridor leading to the DCI's office.

Harris noted her expression.

'OK, OK, I know,' he said.

'One day you'll push it too far.'

'What do you mean "one day"?'

'That's true enough,' said Roberts. 'But don't say I didn't warn you. Anyway, do you trust Jason Craig?'

'Not sure.' Harris held up the statement. 'This could all be baloney. Maybe he'd say anything just to drop James Hall in it. And he could be telling us things about Rad that are already common knowledge. I'm not quite sure what his game is.'

'No, me neither.'

The officers were about to walk into the chief inspector's office when they were approached by Alistair Marshall, his eyes bright with excitement.

'Been looking for you, guv,' said the detective constable.

Harris glanced at Roberts.

'Can't a man bend some rules in peace?' he said.

Despite her reservations, the detective inspector allowed herself a smile.

'Guv?' said Marshall.

'Never mind. Why do you want me?'

'I finally tracked down the girl who was with Annabelle Roper last night,' said Marshall. 'Tracey Malham.'

'That's the one who was with her last time as well, isn't it?' said Roberts.

'Yeah. She reckons that Lee Smedley and another of the boys from Rowan House were there as well.'

'Do we know who?' asked Harris.

'Danny Cairns. He fences most of the stuff that Smedley nicks in the break-ins but we've never been able to prove it. According to Tracey, they were all smoking dope on the wasteland behind the tyre place.'

'And were they there when she died?' asked Harris.

He led them into the office, where they were greeted enthusiastically by the dogs, who had been snoozing in their customary position beneath the radiator. Harris sat down at his desk and reached into his top drawer for some treats, which he flicked towards the animals.

'Tracey is adamant that she wasn't,' said Marshall. 'She reckons that she went home at half eight but that the boys were still there with Annabelle. Says she doesn't know what happened after she left.'

'And do you believe her?' asked Harris. 'I mean, she's not exactly the most reliable of witnesses, is she? Not stringing you a line?'

'I don't think so. She seemed pretty shaken up by Annabelle's death.'

'OK, fair enough.' Harris gave him an approving nod. 'I think we are finally starting to make sense of things. Good work.'

'Thank you, guv. Me and Alison were going to go over to Rowan House and bring Danny Cairns in, if you think it's the right thing to do?'

'Go for it,' said Harris. 'He's got a lot of explaining to do. Oh, and get someone to keep an eye on the wasteland, will you? You never know.'

'You want it searched?' asked Marshall.

'Not yet. Observations for the moment. It's clearly somewhere the kids go.'

'Will do.' Marshall headed for the door, then turned back. 'Oh, and Ellie Cross's mother is in reception. Says she wants to know what's happening.'

'I sent a couple of officers round to see her earlier,' said Gillian Roberts. 'Didn't want her getting her news off the telly.'

'I know but now she says that she will only talk to the governor,' said Marshall. 'Reception told her that you were busy and to come back later but she refused to go. Been there for the best part of an hour, apparently.'

'OK,' said Harris. 'Tell reception that I'm on my way.'

Marshall walked out into the corridor.

'It's the conversation I've been dreading,' said Harris. 'I mean, how do you explain how you let another kid die just four weeks after her daughter?'

'I'm not sure that's the way to look at it. We did everything we could after Ellie died.'

'Did we, though?' said Harris. He shook his head. 'This is a small community and it should not have been beyond us to find out who was bringing MDMA in, Gillian.'

'Yes, but it's not like we didn't try,' protested Roberts. 'You've seen the overtime bill. Think how many searches of lockers we did at the school and we talked to every one of our low-level dealers. All we turned up was cannabis.'

'Nevertheless, I can't help feeling that we should have done more.'

'I'm not sure what else we could have done,' said Roberts. She sounded defensive; she had been in charge of the inquiry. 'The kids weren't saying anything, remember. They've only just started talking since Annabelle died.'

'Fair point,' said Harris. He noticed her expression. 'And I'm not criticising you, Gillian. I'm not criticising anyone. All I'm saying is that I think we might have overlooked something. A piece of the jigsaw.'

Roberts nodded; the comment had reassured her slightly and, if she was honest with herself, she had been thinking the same thing, particularly in the hours following the death of Annabelle Roper.

'Maybe it'll change now,' she said. 'I think what happened last night has given a lot of the kids a real jolt. My boys were pretty upset when I rang them during lunch break. I don't think it'll be long before we get a breakthrough.'

'Somehow,' said Harris, standing up, 'I don't think that will make Maureen Cross feel much better. Or the Ropers, for that matter. We owed it to them to keep their children safe and we failed.'

He strode out into the corridor and headed in the direction of reception. Roberts stood in the office for a few moments then glanced down at the dogs, who were staring expectantly at her.

'Who says that your owner doesn't do empathy?' she murmured.

Chapter fourteen

'How come this has been allowed to happen again, Chief Inspector?' asked Maureen Cross.

Allowed. The word used by David Roper earlier in the day. The word was loaded with recrimination although the tone of Maureen's voice was not accusatory, more bewildered, thought Jack Harris as he stared at her across the interview room table. He did not see a woman seeking to condemn, rather a mother seeking answers about the death of a daughter. Maureen was a slight woman but it seemed to the detective that she had grown smaller since he last saw her.

Grief, he thought, casting his mind back to David Roper's fury, to Glenis's heartbroken tears and her hands constantly twisting and untwisting the handkerchief, affects people in different ways. Except the inspector knew only too well that, for all their different responses, all three of them had something in common, they were all parents who desperately wanted him to assure them that the person responsible for their child's death would be brought to book, that they had not died in vain. Jack Harris was acutely aware that he could not promise that to any of them. Not yet anyway.

'We're doing everything we can,' he said.

Harris cursed inwardly. He knew that it sounded evasive. Lame. The kind of thing that someone would proffer up as a weak excuse when they knew that they didn't have the answers. He hated the way it made him look; he detested not being in control.

'You said that last time.' Maureen gave him a hard look. This time the tone of voice was harsher. Resentful. 'But they're just words, aren't they, Chief Inspector?'

'No, of course—'

'Nothing is actually happening, is it? I mean, if it was, Annabelle Roper would not be dead, would she? The MDMA would not be out there, would it?'

'There's not a person in this police station who does not want whoever supplied the drugs to the girls brought to book,' said Harris. 'They have been working round the clock, Maureen, you have to believe me when I tell you that.'

'I'm sure that's true but nothing has happened, has it? Except another girl has died.'

'I wish I could tell you more,' said Harris. He thought of his conversations with Mel Garside. 'But take it from me, Maureen, we *are* getting closer to the people who brought the MDMA to Levton Bridge. It might not look like it from the outside, but we *are* making progress. Hopefully, we will have something to say very soon.'

'How soon?'

She looked at him keenly, the light of hope in her eyes. Harris hesitated; like all investigators, he had always shied away from making promises that he was not sure he could deliver. It was his mantra to young detectives; he'd delivered the speech to Alison Butterfield and Alistair Marshall on their first days in CID but something about Maureen's expression drove him to break his own rule.

'Tomorrow,' he said. 'Hopefully, I will have something to tell you tomorrow. There have been developments.'

'Are they connected to Annabelle's death? Do you think the person that gave the drugs to Ellie did the same with her?'

'It's a distinct possibility. Tell me, was Ellie friends with Annabelle?'

'They knew each other but I wouldn't have said they were that close, really. I never saw them together. Not that I knew much about Ellie's life – you know what teenagers are like.'

'I'm learning fast.'

'I imagine you are.' Maureen gave a knowing smile. 'You don't have any children of your own, I take it?'

'I don't, no.'

'There's a lot to learn when you do.'

'So people keep telling me.'

'You never stop worrying about them. You want to keep them safe but you can't always do it.' Maureen was silent for a few moments. 'The officers that came to see me said that you believe Annabelle was force-fed the drugs. Is that true?'

'We believe so, yes.'

'So, it's different from Ellie.'

'In some ways. There was no sign that Ellie took the drugs under duress but we think they had both taken MDMA and in a town where the main drug in circulation is cannabis that's pretty significant.'

'But why would someone force the poor girl to take drugs?' Maureen shook her head in disbelief. 'I mean, who on earth could be capable of doing such a terrible thing?'

'Someone who wanted to make sure that Annabelle did not tell anyone what had been happening. Does the name Lee Smedley mean anything to you?'

'Do you think he's responsible for giving Annabelle the drugs?'

'I can't say for definite,' replied Harris. His tone was more guarded; in a town where every snippet of information had been finding its way onto Facebook, he was reluctant to give away too much. 'Do you know him?'

'Everyone knows Lee Smedley, Chief Inspector. If only by reputation. David Roper says that he's a menace.'

'When did you talk to David Roper?' asked Harris.

'He rang me a few days after Ellie died. Said if I needed anything, I was only to ask.'

'And did you?'

'What could he do?' Maureen's expression assumed a deep sadness. 'He wasn't going to bring Ellie back, was he?'

'What kind of help did he have in mind?'

'Legal stuff, I think.'

'Hardly the time to tout for work,' said Harris.

'I appreciate that your job must make you cynical, but I prefer to think that it was a genuine offer.'

'Maybe. Going back to Lee Smedley, were he and Ellie friends?'

'I answered these questions when your officers asked them last time, Chief Inspector. After she died.'

'I know you did but maybe you have remembered something that could be of use,' said Harris. It sometimes happens when people have had time to reflect.'

'Oh, I've had time to reflect, alright,' she said bitterly. 'I've done nothing else but if they were friends, Ellie never told me. I very much doubt that they were. The only time she did mention Lee Smedley, it was to say that he was bad news. He'd got into a fight with some lad in the playground. One of Ellie's friends. Broke his nose.'

'And Danny Cairns?' asked Harris. 'Did Ellie ever mention him?'

'Not really, although I always wondered if he had a thing for her. He came to the house a couple of times but I don't think she was that interested. I'm not sure she would want to go out with a friend of Lee Smedley's anyway. But, like I told Alistair Marshall last time, she was very secretive about her life, was Ellie.'

'I gather they all are.'

'Parents only get told what the kids want them to know, Chief Inspector, and if I ever did ask questions, she accused me of prying and it ended in a row. I did not even know that she was taking drugs. Can you believe that?' Maureen shook her head. 'You'd think a mother would at least know that.'

Harris thought of the long hours of fruitless investigation that had followed Ellie's death, of the exasperation frequently expressed by both Alison Butterfield and Alistair Marshall that the young people of the town would not offer up any information, even though neither officer had long been out of full-time education themselves and thought their age might allow them to make a connection.

'I can believe it, yes,' said Harris. 'It's starting to change a little with what happened to Annabelle but it's still hard going.'

'This progress you mentioned. Can you tell me anything about it? It really would help if I knew.'

Harris looked at the beseeching expression on her face but still hesitated to reply. He recalled another piece of advice that he gave to young officers: *don't tell them anything that you don't want anyone else to know.*

'I won't tell anyone,' said Maureen, reading his mind.

'Have you heard the phrase "County Lines"?'

'There was a big thing on Radio 4 about it last week. Criminals from cities getting young people to take drugs to small towns. Do you think that's what has been happening here?'

'All I can say is that we are working with officers from other forces.' Harris gave her a hard look. 'But please don't breathe a word of this to anyone, Maureen. If anyone finds out what's happening it could wreck everything.'

'I won't and thank you for telling me. It makes me feel a little better.' She reached out across the table and lightly touched his hand. 'I wish you luck. For Ellie's sake.'

An image of the children's bodies in the forest clearing in Kosovo flashed into the inspector's mind again.

'For all their sakes,' he said.

Chapter fifteen

It was mid-evening and Alistair Marshall and Alison Butterfield had been sitting in their car for half an hour, parked alongside the wasteland behind the tyre workshop in Ronaldsway Road, on the fringes of Levton Bridge town centre. They had taken over from the preceding surveillance team half an hour previously but nothing was moving and now the summer sun was starting to sink below the horizon and the shadows were lengthening. And Alison Butterfield was growing restless.

'This is a waste of time,' she said.

'I'll let you tell the governor that. I'm sure that he'd value your expert opinion.'

'Well, it is, Alistair. I mean, isn't it?'

'You never learn, do you?' said Marshall. 'The last time you said something like that, we ended up catching that gang from Liverpool that were screwing the farms. If you'd had your way, we'd have been in the pub.'

'That was different. We'd got good intel on them. God knows what Jack Harris thinks we are going to achieve hanging around here.'

'I am sure he has his reasons.'

'Come on, Alistair,' said Butterfield. The constable's refusal to engage in conversation had irked her. 'There's no way that they are going to return here after everything that's happened, are they? These kids are not stupid, you know. We could wait here all night and come up with nothing. The DCI should have let us go with your idea and conduct a search of...'

Her voice tailed off when a figure appeared on the far side of the wasteland.

'Care to finish that sentence?' asked Marshall. He turned away, hoping that she could not see his grin.

'How does he do it?' said Butterfield. She sank down in her seat so that the young man could not see her. 'I mean, how does the governor know these things?'

'Because he's been there and done it a thousand times,' said Marshall, also sitting lower. 'It's why the sarge is always on at you to watch your mouth when you talk to him. Sometimes you've just got to smile sweetly and do as you are told. You've got to know how to play the game with the governor.'

'Smart arse.' The constable stared across the wasteland, screwing up her eyes so that she could better see the young man's features. 'That's Danny Cairns, isn't it?'

'I reckon so, yes.'

The officers had been looking for the teenager for several hours before taking over the surveillance duty. When they had called at Rowan House earlier in the evening, none of the duty staff knew where he was. Or at least, that's what they told the sceptical detectives. Both officers sensed a strong feeling of resentment at their presence after the day's events and even staff members who had previously been co-operative were distant and evasive.

After leaving Rowan House, the detectives had searched Cairns' usual haunts without finding him but now, with the evening light starting to fade, he had broken cover.

'Wonder what he's doing here?' said Butterfield.

'I think we can offer a pretty good guess.'

Cairns took a final furtive look round to ensure that he was not being observed, looked harder at their car before satisfying himself that it was empty, then set off across the wasteland towards a tumbledown outbuilding standing in the lee of the wall that ran behind the tyre workshop. He disappeared inside for a moment then emerged clutching a small package.

'OK, let's nick him,' said Marshall.

They were about to get out of the car when a young girl appeared on the far side of the wasteland. After also glancing round furtively, she started to make her way across the rubble towards Cairns.

'Tracey Malham,' said Marshall. 'Now, what the hell is she doing here, I wonder? She said that she hardly knows Danny.'

'Clearly, she's lying,' said Butterfield.

'Clearly she is. So much for being upset about Annabelle.'

They watched as the teenagers approached each other and engaged in conversation. They had their backs to the detectives so the officers could not see precisely what was happening but it appeared that the packet was being handed over.

'Danny must be her supplier,' said Butterfield.

'Well, whatever he is, I've seen enough,' said Marshall.

The officers got out of the car and started to walk across the wasteland. Cairns saw them first, gave a cry of alarm and began to run. Tracey did the same, in the opposite direction.

'You get her!' shouted Marshall and set off after Cairns.

The detective caught up with the teenager just before Cairns reached the road. Cairns whirled round and lashed out with his fist. Alistair Marshall expertly swayed out of the way and grabbed Cairns by the shoulder, spinning him round so that he staggered. A knee buckled and the constable twisted the teenager's arm behind his back, forced him to the ground, and made to secure his wrists with the handcuffs from his belt.

'Ow, you're fucking hurting me!' squealed Cairns as he tried to break free. 'I'll have you for police brutality!'

'Right bunch of barrack room lawyers, aren't you?' said Marshall as he snapped on the cuffs then loosened his grip slightly. 'Always telling us that you know your rights. If you stop struggling, I'll stop hurting you.'

Cairns swore but stopped resisting.

'That's better,' said Marshall.

The constable turned to watch as Butterfield marched a glum-faced Tracey Malham over to them. She was also handcuffed.

'Hardly know Danny then?' said Marshall. He gave her a hard look. 'All lies. He's only your bloody dealer.'

Malham glowered at him.

'I ain't saying nowt,' she said.

'You don't need to after what we've just seen,' said Marshall. 'All that stuff about how you could have saved Annabelle's life was just an act, was it, Tracey?'

'Fuck off.'

'Charming. I suppose you thought if you told me that Danny and Lee were with her last night, we'd turn a blind eye to your drug-taking, did you? You're a piece of work, you really are.'

'You said you wouldn't tell! You said that no one would find out.'

'That was before I realised that you were lying through your teeth.'

Cairns glared at Malham.

'You stiffed me?' he said angrily. 'Bitch!'

Cairns lunged at her but Marshall was too quick for him and tightened his grip again. Cairns cried out in pain.

'I'll have you for that!' said the teenager, trying to wriggle free again. 'Police brutality, that's what—'

'Oh, change the record, will you?' said Marshall wearily. He glanced at the packet in Butterfield's hand, then at Cairns. 'What's that then?'

'Cannabis. I had nothing to do with them deaths. I told you that.'

'Danny, if you told me it was raining, I'd stick my hand out of the window to make sure,' said Marshall.

He took the packet from Butterfield and opened it. He sighed as he saw the contents.

'Cannabis,' he said in disgust. 'Bloody cannabis.'

'I told you,' said Cairns. 'I don't deal in MDMA.'

'Right little angel, aren't you?' Marshall thought back to Ellie Cross lying lifeless on her bed, her system overwhelmed by the drug. And to the pictures he had seen of Annabelle Roper sprawled in the copse. 'Come on, both of you, down the station.'

'Why?' protested Cairns. 'It's just a bit of weed. Aren't you supposed to let us off with a warning?'

'Not this time, sunbeam. There's too many questions need answering. And this time we want the truth.'

* * *

Ten minutes later, the officers were taking the teenagers in through the back door of the police station when Jack Harris approached along the corridor. The inspector glanced at Malham then gave Marshall an enquiring look.

'Tracey Malham,' explained the constable. 'We found Danny selling her drugs at Ronaldsway Road. Cannabis.'

'So much for her not stringing you a line then,' said Harris.

He gave a slight smile as he saw Marshall's crestfallen expression. The inspector headed off down the corridor.

'Come and see me when you've finished, will you?' he said over his shoulder. 'I'd love to hear all about it.'

When Harris had gone, Butterfield gave Marshall an impish grin.

'What was that about knowing how to play the game?' she said.

Alistair Marshall gave her a sour look but said nothing. Danny Cairns sniggered.

Chapter sixteen

It had just gone ten and Jack Harris had put on his coat and was about to leave his office at the end of as long and wearisome a day as he could remember since his return to Levton Bridge, when Alistair Marshall appeared at the door.

'You still here?' said the inspector.

'You wanted to know how it went with the kids.'

'Ah, yes.' Harris took his coat off, sat down behind his desk and gestured for the constable to take a seat. 'So?'

'Nothing,' said Marshall.

'Hardly the kind of thorough update I would have liked to hear from one of my detectives. So what happened?'

Marshall sighed; he had been dreading the encounter. Word had spread quickly that Harris felt that the team had fallen short on the investigation.

'They didn't change their story one bit,' said the young detective. 'Tracey kept claiming that she knows nothing about MDMA, even when her dad pressed her, and Danny Cairns said virtually nothing. Not that the guy that Rowan House sent with him was very helpful, mind. We're not exactly in their good books.'

'I guess not,' said Harris. He glanced at the wall clock. 'OK, get yourself home. Have another go at them tomorrow, yeah? Maybe the headteacher can persuade them to open up.'

'I wouldn't hold out too much hope,' said Marshall glumly as he stood up. 'No one at that school seems willing to tell us what they know.'

'Don't take it to heart,' said Harris. He gave him a reassuring smile. 'We all have days like this.'

Marshall left the room with an overwhelming feeling of relief; it was like everyone said, you just did not know how Jack Harris would react. Back in his office, the inspector had just started to put his coat on again when his mobile phone rang.

'For fuck's sake,' he growled. 'What now?'

He fished the device out of his jacket pocket and glanced down at the readout. He smiled and took the call.

'Now then,' he said.

'Now then,' said Jenny Armannsson. 'You still at work?'

'Afraid so.'

'I almost didn't ring you. Wondered if you'd gone to bed early, what with the early start tomorrow.'

'Some chance,' said Harris.

'Anyway, I'm just ringing to say good luck in Newcastle.'

'How do you know about that?'

'Leckie told me. Sounds exciting. Bit better than lifting bent accountants.'

'I still think I'll need all the luck I can get.'

Harris put his feet up on the desk. The dogs, who had been following him towards the door when the call came in, settled back down under the radiator with an air of familiar resignation.

'It all looked pretty heavy from what I saw on Sky News.'

'Like you said last night, children change everything. Seeing the body of Annabelle Roper shook me up a little, if the truth be told.'

'Really? You've seen bodies before, though. Dead kids, too, I imagine. It's not like you to react like this.'

'I know but this one feels different.'

'What do you mean, different?' asked Jenny.

Harris did not reply. Sitting there is his office, he was transported back to Kosovo. To the clearing. To the sight of soldiers crying as they thought of their own children. Harris frowned; his efforts to control the flashbacks, to suppress the feelings, were failing.

'Jack?' said Jenny as the silence lengthened. 'You still there?'

Her voice seemed to come from afar and the inspector realised that the hand holding the mobile had slipped down his side. He put the device back to his ear.

'Yeah, sorry, love,' he said. 'Dropped the phone.'

'You OK?'

'Yeah, fine. Why do you ask?'

'You've not sounded yourself for a few days now.'

'Just a bit tired,' said Harris. 'Today has not helped.'

'You said that this one felt different. What does that mean?'

'I blame you.'

'Me?'

'Yeah. Making me think about having kids.' Harris hesitated. 'Look, Jenny, I really don't want kids, not yet anyway. If the past few weeks has taught me anything – re-taught me – it's that I don't do children.'

'No, me neither.'

'You don't? But I thought...'

'Of course, I don't,' she said. 'Why would I want kids? I've got my career to think about. It was just an idle comment. There's no way I want any more mewling people in my life at the moment, thank you very much.

I've got enough with the guys on my squad. God, I hate doing the rotas.'

'Glad we agree,' said Harris. Relief flooded his body.

'We do.' Her turn to hesitate. 'On some things anyway.'

Harris knew what was coming. He'd guessed she would raise the subject and that it wouldn't take long. The realisation had not helped his mood. Things were moving too quickly.

'What do you mean?' he asked.

'Given the way this conversation is going, I'm not sure if it's the right time to mention it,' she said, 'but a job advert was posted today – a promotion that I quite fancy.'

'What is it?' asked Harris but he did not need to be told; he'd seen the advert as well. Knew she'd bring it up.

'Uniform Chief Inspector. Based in Roxham. I thought that you might have mentioned it, actually.'

'Sorry, must have slipped my mind with everything going on.'

'Understandable.' She didn't sound convinced. 'So, what do you think, Jack? Should I go for it? We'd be based in different police stations, if that's what's worrying you.'

'I know.'

'And it would mean that we wouldn't have to do all that travelling to see each other. I am getting heartily sick of the M6 roadworks.'

'Isn't everybody.'

'You still don't sound sure, though.'

'Do you really want to go back into uniform?' he asked.

'You have to if you want to get on, you know that.'

'I guess, but Roxham's hardly the bright lights, Jenny. It would be a hell of a shock after living in Manchester. They think a trip to the Golden Palace takeaway is the height of fine dining here.'

'Levton Bridge is not much better,' she said. 'But you manage.'

Harris thought of his cottage on the hill, the row of empty whisky bottles lined up in the shed, the long solitary walks with the dogs across the moors.

'I'm different,' he said.

'So, you don't think I should go for it then?' She sounded disappointed. 'Is that what you're saying?'

'No, of course it's not. It's just that it feels like it's a big decision. I mean, presumably you'd want to move in with me?'

'It would make sense,' she said. 'I won't go for it if you don't want me to, but now's the time to say.'

Harris thought for a moment and made the decision that had been coming for six months. Surprised himself.

'No,' he said. 'You go for it.'

'Sure?'

'Yeah, sure. I'll even put a word in for you, if you think it would help you get the job.'

'Now I know that you don't want me to get it,' she said.

Harris chuckled then was silent for a few moments. It felt like he'd made a big decision. Time to make another. Take Jenny into his confidence; she deserved to know why he had been so distracted over recent days.

'Tell me,' he said, 'what do you know about war crimes investigations?'

* * *

It was just after midnight when the mud-spattered decorator's van pulled up at the end of the road on the Newcastle housing estate and the driver switched off the engine and cut the lights. As he did so, a car at the far end of the road flicked its headlights and eased itself round the corner and out of sight. In the van, the two Northumbria Police Organised Crime Unit surveillance officers settled down for their shift, their task being to keep an eye on the house occupied by Rad until the raid team arrived at first light. As Jack Harris had suspected, the address supplied by Jason Craig was already well known to Mel Garside and her team and had been under constant surveillance as final preparations for the raids were made.

Within half an hour, the last of the house lights in the street had been extinguished, all except in the target property, a run-down semi-detached house where the front room window was still illuminated behind thick curtains.

'Our Rad's working late,' said the van driver, an experienced detective sergeant.

'Probably getting his next delivery ready,' said his passenger, a young detective constable. 'Any word on this kid that Levton Bridge want for the murder?'

'No, nothing yet. No one even knows if he's over here. Right little tearaway, by all accounts. Only fifteen but a real hard-case.'

'Sounds it. What about this DCI that is after him? What's his story? Bit urban for a woollyback like him, isn't it?'

'Jack Harris is anything but a woollyback.' The driver glanced across at his colleague. 'And you'd do well to remember that he hates the phrase. He's chinned folk for calling him it. There's plenty of folks who have regretted under-estimating Jack Harris, you take it from me.'

'Yeah, but Levton Bridge? I went there on holiday once. Took Mary and the kids for a week and we were back by the Wednesday. It's at the arse end of beyond, fuck all to do and it pissed down all the time. Hardly going to be a hot-shot, is he?'

The driver allowed himself a knowing smile.

'Do you remember five years ago when Greater Manchester broke up that cocaine gang that had turned over seven million in less than a year?' he said. 'The one with links to the Colombian cartel? Made all the headlines.'

'Yeah. What of it?'

'That was your woollyback cop when he worked in Manchester.'

'Really?'

'Yeah, really. Harris and his team had been after them for six months and it was the fourth major gang they had busted in three years. Harris got himself a special commendation and, according to Mel Garside, drug trafficking in Manchester went down sixty percent.'

'So, if he's such a hot-shot, what's he doing in a backwater like Levton Bridge?'

'According to the governor, he missed walking his dogs on the hills. Takes them everywhere with him, even on jobs. There's even word that he might bring them tomorrow.'

'Jesus Christ.'

'I told you, it's woe betide anyone who under-estimates Jack Harris. Doesn't suffer fools gladly, that one. And, according to the governor, he's not averse to bending a few rules, neither. Tomorrow should be interesting.'

The passenger was about to reply when a movement at the other end of the street caught his eye. A lithe young man wearing a black T-shirt and combat trousers emerged from the shadows and loped effortlessly towards Rad's house. The watching officers recalled the photograph they had been shown at that evening's briefing by Mel Garside.

'That looks like the Smedley boy,' said the sergeant. 'Jack Harris *will* be pleased.'

Smedley disappeared into the house and the officers settled down in their seats; it was going to be a long night.

Chapter seventeen

Shortly after 2:30am, Jack Harris emerged from his hillside home, dogs at his heels, and headed along the path leading across the field. He illuminated the way with a torch but his main guide was instinct and he was steady of foot on a route that he and the animals had walked many times before in the years since the inspector had finished renovating the former shepherd's cottage.

More than once, the inspector paused to listen to the heavy silence of the night, nodding his head in appreciation of the seclusion. He sighed; always a man with a dark side, his thoughts were troubled and it seemed to him that problem was piling upon problem. Confusing thoughts were crowding in on him. His mind went back to the conversation with Jenny; Harris had long valued his solitude and he was not sure how it would feel to share it, not even with someone for whom he held such strong feelings. He was also not sure how Jenny would respond to life on the hill; she'd only been to the cottage once in their year together. However, it had felt good to reveal to someone that he had been approached by prosecutors trying to bring the perpetrators of the massacre in Kosovo to justice.

He peered into the darkness again and sighed. Jack Harris liked life when it was simple: him, the dogs and his beloved hills. Conscious that he was allowing himself to be distracted, he pondered instead the upcoming event in Newcastle. Although the pull of the hills had eventually proved too strong and carried him back to the area in which he had grown up, there were times when he missed the excitement of the city. Missed the big operations, the buzz of taking down the gangs.

Thought of the city made the inspector recall Matty Gallagher and, with a click of the tongue, he turned and he and the dogs headed back to the Land Rover parked outside the cottage. Having loaded the dogs into the back of the vehicle, Harris guided the vehicle down the twisty, rock-strewn track towards the valley road, where he turned left and made the five-mile journey into Levton Bridge. Having navigated the deserted streets of the town, the inspector headed out onto the moors and down the valley to Roxham. Shortly after 3:30am, he picked up a bleary Matty Gallagher from the terraced house he shared with his wife.

'What kind of time do you call this?' grumbled the sergeant as he got into the vehicle.

Harris said nothing but drove out of Roxham and onto the eastbound moorland road. As the vehicle covered the silent miles, Gallagher stared gloomily out of the window into the darkness, which was streaked with the first glimmers of morning light. Unlike his boss, he had never appreciated North Pennine nights; he missed his previous life in the bustling streets of London. Matty Gallagher was a man who liked being in the midst of people, liked the glow of streetlamps and the sound of voices.

'I should still be in bed,' he said as he struggled to see anything out of the window.

Still, Harris did not reply. Gallagher was used to many silent journeys with the uncommunicative inspector but something told him that this was different.

'Still bugged about having children?' he asked eventually.

'You never give up, do you?'

'Nope. So, is that what's still bugging you?'

'No, not really. Jenny wants to go for that chief inspector's job in Roxham. Move in with me.'

'And what did you say?'

'I said yes.'

'And is that what you meant?'

'I'm not sure,' said Harris. 'I'm not exactly the easiest person to live with.'

'Surely not.'

Harris allowed himself a slight smile. His attempts to be grumpy around the sergeant rarely lasted long; if he was honest with himself, he appreciated Gallagher's efforts to lighten the mood on occasion.

'Want to talk about it?' asked Gallagher after a few moments.

'Not really.' The inspector's appreciation only went so far.

When it was clear that Harris was not about to elaborate on his thoughts, Gallagher went back to staring out of the window into the darkness, watching as the light strengthened over the hills. He contemplated the morning's activities. The thought cheered him up; he loved being back in the city and, like the inspector, relished the excitement of big operations.

'Should be good this morning,' he said.

'Should be,' said Harris. He was relieved to get back onto ground where he felt more comfortable. 'Mel reckons that they are going to raid twelve houses. They've got seventeen targets on their list. Including Rad.'

'Excellent. I fancy kicking a few doors in. It's felt like we've not been doing anything over the past few weeks. Not enough, anyway. Did that address Jason Craig gave us check out?'

'It did, yes, but he wasn't exactly giving anything much away. I rang Mel last night and she said it's pretty common knowledge that's where Rad runs his operation from.'

'You had any more thoughts on Craig?'

'I'm still struggling to work him out,' said Harris. 'Gillian agrees. He's playing a game but we don't know the rules.'

'You kept him in overnight, I think?'

'Yeah, I thought it for the best. He bleated on about his human rights and his solicitor tried to persuade me to change my mind but the lad's a loose cannon. The last thing we wanted was him going back to Newcastle and having another crack at Rad. Or, worse still, letting on that we are interested in him. Mel would never forgive me if we bollocksed up her operation. They've been setting it up for months and some of her team already think that we're a bunch of woollybacks.'

'You'll put them right. Any word on Lee Smedley?'

'Mel texted me just after midnight to say that their surveillance guys had seen him at Rad's house.'

'Could leave us with some awkward questions to answer if it turns out that he had something to do with the deaths. The guy who was responsible under our noses all the time. Especially if the media get hold of it. They're always looking for new angles.'

Harris thought back to the previous evening's encounter with Maureen Cross. *How come this has been allowed to happen again, Chief Inspector?*

'Frankly, I'm not sure what answer we could give, Matty lad,' he said. 'One thing's for sure, we can't afford to let Smedley slip through our fingers again.'

Silence settled on the vehicle again. It was broken by Gallagher. It was always broken by Gallagher – the sergeant disliked silence.

'Alistair get anywhere with the kids last night?' he asked.

'Not really. They both stuck to their story.'

'And what *is* their story?' asked Gallagher.

'Tracey kept saying she had no idea how the girls got hold of the MDMA and Danny Cairns insisted he was only pushing weed. He says that Annabelle was alive when he and Smedley left her and they don't know how she got to the copse. And he's adamant that her death is nothing to do with Smedley.'

'I might have been tempted to believe him until Smedley turned up in Newcastle. Someone is bringing the MDMA over here and, for my money, Smedley has gone to the head of the queue.'

'He certainly has,' said Harris. He glanced across at the sergeant. 'Too many secrets, Matty lad.'

'You're right there,' said Gallagher.

Chapter eighteen

The morning light was washing the hills with a faint glow as the Land Rover left the Pennines behind and dropped down onto the dual carriageway leading into Newcastle. As the detectives entered the outskirts of the city, Matty Gallagher stared out of the window at the rows of houses, the corner shops, the public houses, and felt his spirits lifting. Memories of his days in London stirred; as always whenever he left the valley, he had a strong sense that he had rejoined the rest of the world.

'Looking forward to this,' he said, rubbing his hands together.

'So you said.'

They were the first words the inspector had uttered for thirty minutes and his brooding silence following their conversation had done little for Gallagher's mood. The more the sergeant thought about it, the more he became convinced that there was something that Harris was not telling him. But, like everyone else at Levton Bridge Police Station, he did not feel that he had the kind of relationship with the inspector to properly question him on the issue. Indeed, Gallagher felt that he had already pushed it as far as he dared. The rest was up to Harris, he decided.

As the morning light strengthened, the inspector guided the Land Rover through deserted Newcastle streets, the only sound in the vehicle the occasional instruction from the sat nav, until eventually, just as Gallagher wondered if they were leaving the city again, Harris turned off onto an industrial estate which was populated with drab workshops standing silent and in darkness. After five minutes, the sat nav announced that they had reached their destination and Harris pulled up outside a non-descript grey-clad, windowless building. It bore no identifying marks but this was the home of the Organised Crime Unit to which Mel Garside and her team were assigned.

'Ah, the glamour of police work,' said Gallagher, eying the building without much enthusiasm.

A uniformed officer at the gatehouse checked their credentials and pointed them to the visitors' section of the car park. Harris parked up, the detectives got out of the vehicle and the inspector let the dogs out of the back.

'Are you sure you can take them in?' asked Gallagher dubiously.

'They'll be fine.'

The two officers and the dogs headed for the front of the building and Harris pressed an intercom to be let in. The door swung open and they walked into a brightly lit reception area. The young girl behind the desk smiled.

'DI Garside said you might bring them,' she said, gesturing to the dogs. 'She suggested that I look after them while you're out. Are they hungry?'

'Always,' said Harris.

'I've got a nice treat for them – bit of steak.' The receptionist picked up her desk phone. 'They're here, ma'am.'

A couple of minutes later, a small dark-haired woman wearing a dark suit emerged from a side door and gave the detectives a welcoming beam.

'Gentlemen,' she said. 'Welcome to civilisation.'

'Hello, Mel,' said Harris as they shook hands. 'Good to see you again.'

'And you. Hiya, Matty. Good to meet you at long last.' She shook the sergeant's hand as well, then nodded towards Harris. 'He still a pain in the arse?'

Gallagher grinned.

'Pretty much,' he said.

Garside looked at the dogs.

'You have no idea how many strings I had to pull to let you bring them,' she said.

Harris nodded his appreciation, the receptionist produced feeding bowls from behind the desk and Garside led the detectives through the security door, up a set of stairs and into a briefing room that was already full of officers. A number of them sneaked glances in the direction of the new arrivals; word of Jack Harris's reputation had gone before him, largely spread by Mel Garside and her senior officers who had warned their younger, more headstrong colleagues not to under-estimate the officers from the valley. And not to crack jokes about sheep...

As the Levton Bridge detectives crossed the room, a tall dark-haired man in uniform stood up, detached himself from a small group of officers and walked over with a broad smile on his face. Graham Leckie, a constable with Greater Manchester Police, was one of the inspector's few close friends, the two men having met when Harris worked in the city. Even though Harris eventually left Manchester to return home to Levton Bridge, he and Leckie still talked on a regular basis because, in addition to having bonded over a love of wildlife and fishing trips, the constable worked in force intelligence. Because the valley often witnessed crimes committed by criminals travelling north, the flow of information in both directions was constant.

'How the hell are you, Hawk?' asked Leckie as they shook hands. 'And when are we going to get that fishing trip on?'

'I know, I know,' said Harris with a sigh. 'Things keep getting in the way. You know how it is, Graham. As for how I am, I'll be better when we've got our hands on Lee Smedley.'

'Yeah, he sounds like a real crackerjack.' Leckie extended a hand to Gallagher. 'Hiya, Matty. He still a pain in the arse?'

Gallagher grinned and Harris feigned disapproval.

'You lot need a new scriptwriter,' he said. 'That's what Mel said.'

'I didn't say I was original.' Leckie grinned. 'Still seeing young Jenny, I hear. It's serious then, is it?'

Before Harris could reply, Mel Garside walked to the front of the room and the gathering fell silent. Harris and Gallagher took their seats next to Leckie.

'Thank you for turning out so early,' said Garside. 'I think you all know why we are here.'

She turned to look at a board on which was pinned a series of photographs, a mixture of shaven-headed men with flattened noses and crooked teeth, a number that offered a more presentable image and several gaunt, hard-boned women who stared out into the room with narrowed eyes. On the far end of the row, Garside had pinned a photograph of Lee Smedley, emailed by Gallagher the previous evening. Even in a photograph, the teenager's eyes seemed to glint with animal cunning.

'Operation Rapier,' said Garside. She tapped the board. 'Nick this little lot and we punch a big hole in drug dealing across not just our city but further afield. On that note, can I extend a welcome to our visitors, DCI Jack Harris and DS Matty Gallagher from Levton Bridge and PC Graham Leckie from Greater Manchester Police.'

A murmur rippled round the room. Gallagher and Leckie gave nods of appreciation. Jack Harris did not acknowledge the comment. He rarely did in such situations but stared ahead stony-faced; he knew what some city officers thought about colleagues from rural areas and had long since concluded that the tough exterior served him best in such situations.

'They are here,' said Garside, 'because, like the Northumbria force, their areas have seen young people dying from drug overdoses over recent months. I am sure that you all saw the television coverage yesterday about the fifteen-year-old who died in Levton Bridge. The second death in a little over a month, I think, Jack?'

'I am afraid so.'

'Do you want to say anything before we split off for the individual briefings?'

'Please.' Harris walked to the front of the room.

'Just to say,' he began, 'that, like Mel says, we've got two teenage girls dead after taking drugs and I think that your guy Rad is to blame. I am worried that there could be more deaths unless we put a stop to it.'

'Anything you want to say about Lee Smedley?' asked Garside.

Harris walked over to rest a hand on the teenager's photograph.

'Only that you should not under-estimate him just because he's only fifteen years old,' said the inspector. 'He's a slippery character and he is perfectly capable of having it away on his toes. He's very athletic, runs like the wind and has plenty of animal cunning.'

Harris thought of the scratches on Annabelle Roper's body.

'And we have reason to believe that he is dangerous,' he added. 'In addition to drug trafficking, we want to talk to him in connection with the murder of one of our girls.'

Harris sat down.

'Thank you, Jack,' said Garside. She looked round the room. 'Before you are briefed individually, let me say one thing. If our intelligence is right, Rad and his gang are responsible for moving drugs all across the north. We can connect them not just with Levton Bridge through Lee Smedley but with a dozen market towns like it. I cannot stress enough that the effect of their activities on these communities has been devastating. In addition to the two girls Jack mentioned and the ones in the Manchester area, we believe they are responsible for deaths in several of our market towns so I want this morning's operation done right.'

Her gaze ranged around the room.

'I don't want anyone getting away,' she continued. 'And be careful, there are reports that some of them carry knives. They may even have firearms, so if in doubt let the heavy mob go in first. Each team will be accompanied by firearms officers and let them lead if you think it's necessary. I don't want any heroes, particularly not dead ones.'

Murmurs rippled round the room.

'And one more thing,' she said. Her voice had changed. It was less business-like, softer, more human. Sombre. 'A lot of you are parents of teenagers – I've got a fourteen-year-old and a fifteen-year-old myself – and we all know what we would think if someone tried to sell them drugs.'

This time, the murmurs were louder. The atmosphere was growing in the room, there was a real sense of tension, a feeling that something big was about to happen. A job that had to be done and done well. Both Harris and Gallagher were relishing the occasion; it felt good to be doing something positive after a month in which they had felt increasingly impotent and embattled.

'What I am saying,' continued Garside, 'is that you leave your emotions at the door to this briefing room. I don't want anyone cutting corners and I don't want to hear that anyone has assaulted a suspect. I want this done right.'

She turned to look at the row of photographs.

'The last thing I want is for us to give some fast-talking lawyer the opportunity to get any of this lot off on a technicality. I want this collection of beauties locked up for a long time. OK, let's do it.'

There was a scraping of chairs and loud voices of agreement as the gathering broke up and the teams headed for their individual briefings. Harris glanced at Gallagher.

'Excellent,' he said.

Gallagher nodded; it was going to be a good day.

Chapter nineteen

With the briefings completed, a fleet of police minibuses and patrol cars emerged from the secure yard behind the building shortly after 5:30am. On board were a mixture of officers in full assault gear, firearms teams and plainclothes detectives. Mel Garside was in the passenger seat of the lead minibus, which also contained Harris and Gallagher. As the convoy wound its way through the city, the atmosphere in the vehicle was solemn, each officer alone with their thoughts. They knew how much planning had gone into the operation and no one wanted to make a mistake. Matty Gallagher's eyes were bright as he peered out of the window at the deserted early morning streets. Jack Harris stared at the back of his seat.

After ten minutes, the lead vehicle and a patrol car peeled off from the main convoy and made their way to the street where Rad lived. They pulled up next to the van containing the surveillance officers and Garside rolled down her window.

'Anything?' she asked in a quiet voice.

'No, all quiet,' said the driver.

'Rad and Smedley still in there?'

'We believe so, yes.'

Garside nodded her satisfaction and wound the window back up. Over the next few minutes as the vehicles sat with headlights extinguished, different voices came over the radio, announcing when each team was in place. When Garside was satisfied that the last one had reported in, she glanced at the clock on the dashboard then back at Harris, who was sitting just behind her.

'Want to play nice?' she said.

'Ready when you are.'

'OK, let's go and ruin their beauty sleep.' She leaned forward slightly and spoke into the radio. 'Go, go!'

The police vehicles moved quickly to park outside the target house where the members of the team poured out. One officer walked briskly up to the front door, clutching a hydraulic ram.

'Police!' he shouted.

Without waiting for a reply, he smashed the ram into the door. It took three blows to rip the door from its hinges and, amid the sound of tearing timber, the lead officers burst into the house. Warning shouts filled the air and several of the team barged into the living room where they startled a young man who was sleeping on the sofa beneath a thin blanket. Before the bewildered suspect knew what was happening, he had been hauled to his feet, placed in handcuffs and was being led out into the street where he looked in confusion at Harris and Gallagher. Gallagher looked at Harris who shook his head; neither officer recognised the young man.

More members of the team thundered up the stairs, bursting into the bedrooms, in one of which they found a half-naked Rad struggling out of bed. He tried to resist but within seconds rough hands had taken hold of him and he had been overwhelmed and cuffed. A lithe figure dressed in a T-shirt and combat trousers appeared at the entrance to the other bedroom. Evading grasping police hands, he darted down the stairs, taking three stairs at a time. At the bottom, he pushed past another officer and ran into the kitchen at the rear of the house.

'Smedley!' cried Harris.

The inspector ran towards the kitchen, where Smedley was struggling desperately with the key in the back door. As Harris approached, the teenager gave a cry of triumph, wrenched open the door and plunged outside into the pale morning sunshine. Harris followed him and was just in time to see Smedley running at high speed towards the low fence at the bottom of the garden.

'Lee Smedley!' shouted Harris.

Smedley turned, hesitated with one hand on the fence and looked at the inspector in surprise.

'You?' he said. 'What you doing here?'

'You know the answer to that.' Harris took a step forwards and held out a hand. 'Come on, son, you can't run for ever.'

'I ain't giving myself up. You'll only try and pin the deaths of them girls on me and I ain't got nothing to do with that.'

'Then you have nothing to fear.' Harris took a couple of steps closer.

'Don't I?' said Smedley. 'You've got it in for me, everyone knows that. Don't matter what I say. You'll fit me up.'

'Well, you're not exactly an angel, Lee, but you have my word that I won't fit you up.' Harris took another couple of steps. 'If you weren't the one who sold the girls the MDMA, then maybe you know who did?'

Smedley hesitated.

'Come on, son,' said Harris, walking forward again. 'You are only making things worse for yourself.'

'I've never sold MDMA in me life.'

'Then let's get this straightened out.' Harris held out a hand again. 'Come on, Lee, all I want to do is make sure that no more kids die.'

'Sorry,' said Smedley. 'I don't trust cops and I especially don't trust you.'

And with that Smedley leapt over the fence in one smooth movement. A helpless Harris could only watch as he fled across other back gardens, effortlessly hurdling the fences until he reached a side road where he easily evaded the grasping hands of two uniformed officers who had been stationed there to stop escapees. Bursting into the clear, Smedley turned, grinned at the officers, stuck up a finger then vanished into an alleyway. The uniformed officers gave chase but were no match for the fleet-footed teenager and by the time they reached the alleyway he had gone.

Jack Harris strode back to the house with a thunderous look on his face. Reaching the back door, he aimed a furious kick at a dustbin, which toppled over onto its side, spilling its contents. Gallagher appeared at the door and stood on the back step, surveying the used needles, old pizza boxes and beer cans strewn across the path.

'I take it you lost him,' he said.

'Yeah,' said Harris. 'Damn it, damn it, damn it.'

'He can't get far,' said Garside as Harris walked into the kitchen.

Her radio crackled.

'Sorry, ma'am,' said a voice. 'Smedley got away.'

Harris grimaced.

'You were saying?' he said.

'We'll pick him up soon enough,' said Garside.

'You don't know Lee Smedley,' said Gallagher. 'The kid seems able to vanish into thin air.'

'But where can he go?' asked Garside. 'If he stays in Newcastle, we'll lift him soon enough and he can't go back to Levton Bridge, can he?'

'Maybe he'll go back to Blackpool,' said Gallagher as the detectives walked into the hallway.

A plainclothes officer approached them and held up a plastic bag containing a long-bladed knife.

'Found this next to Rad's bed,' he said. 'Thankfully, he was too surprised to go for it.'

'It's enough to send him away on its own,' said Garside. 'Any word from the other teams?'

'All targets acquired, as far as I can make out, ma'am. They're starting the searches now but one of the teams found a handgun lying on a table and there's loads of drugs, apparently. We found a load of heroin and tablets upstairs here as well. Bagged up and ready to go.'

Garside looked at the Levton Bridge detectives.

'Could link to your guy,' she said.

'Could well do,' said Harris. He frowned. 'Although he was absolutely adamant that he doesn't sell MDMA.'

'So, he's lying,' said Gallagher. 'Like you always say, you wouldn't trust Lee Smedley as far as you can throw him. He's hardly going to admit it, is he?'

'Maybe. I mean, we know he was burgling the house in Nightingale Road the night she died, don't we?'

'He could have done both. He'd have been in and out of the house in a matter of minutes.'

'I guess.'

'Hang on,' said Gallagher. 'Are you saying that you believe him?'

'I'm not sure, Matty lad. Maybe he *is* telling the truth.'

'Or more likely he's trying to get us to look elsewhere.'

Harris considered the point for a few moments then nodded.

'Yeah, you're right,' he said. 'I'm not thinking straight. Must be going soft in my old age.'

'Pity he's the only one we didn't pick up,' said Garside. She gave the inspector a crooked grin. 'You could have asked him. In my experience, a couple of hours in an interview room with you can work wonders.'

'Yeah,' replied the inspector. 'Make me feel better, why don't you?'

* * *

They gathered in the main meeting room at Roxham Comprehensive School shortly after 9:00am. It was a large group; the headteacher, form tutor Angie Coulson, detectives Alistair Marshall and Alison Butterfield, Danny Cairns and James Hall from Rowan House, Tracey Malham and her father. He looked furious, Danny Cairns looked bored, the headteacher looked worried.

'Have you had time to think about things?' asked Marshall, looking at the teenagers.

'I told you,' said Cairns. He glared at Tracey Malham; the ill-feeling from the previous evening had not dissipated. 'I don't know about her but I had nothing to do with what happened to them girls.'

Tracey nodded.

'Nothing to do with me,' she said.

'But you *were* dealing drugs,' said Marshall, looking at Cairns then over to Tracey. 'And you were buying the gear from him.'

'It was only a bit of weed,' she said.

'Yeah, it was only a bit of weed,' said Cairns. He looked across the table at Alison Butterfield. 'You saw that for yourself. You both did.'

James Hall intervened, speaking for the first time. He directed his comments to Marshall.

'Look, Constable,' he said. 'I appreciate that you have a job to do but if Danny says he was only dealing cannabis I, for one, believe him. After all, you have no evidence to prove otherwise, do you? And I know it's serious but I'm not sure he'll be locked up for it. Are you?'

Marshall shook his head.

'There you are then,' said Hall.

'So why drag me from fucking work?' said Tracey's father angrily, unable to contain himself no longer. 'Me wages will be docked for this. I mean, Tracey has been stupid but what are we doing here if you aren't going to charge her?'

'Might I remind you that two girls are dead,' said Marshall.

'Don't treat us like idiots, man!' exclaimed the father. 'We all know that but there's nothing to say that my daughter was involved, is there?'

Again, Marshall shook his head. He was acutely aware that he had lost control of the situation.

'And,' continued the father, looking at his daughter, 'if she knew who had sold them girls the drugs, don't you think she would have told you? You don't know, do you, girl?'

Tracey shook her head.

'No,' she said. 'No, I don't.'

'Neither do I,' said Cairns. 'Like I said, I don't do MDMA.'

Marshall looked at Angie Coulson.

'What do you think?' he asked.

'If they say they don't know who killed Annabelle, they don't know.'

Silence settled on the room for a few moments, eventually broken by James Hall.

'It would seem,' he said, looking round the table, 'that we have reached something of an impasse, ladies and gentlemen. Perhaps now would be a good time to adjourn?'

'I agree,' said the headteacher. 'And I'd thank people to keep the details of this meeting confidential, please. The events of recent days have unsettled the pupils enough as it is and are doing incalculable damage to the school. The governors are very concerned.'

He looked relieved as everyone nodded and stood up to leave.

'Unless we find something else out, that is,' said Marshall, an edge to his voice. He looked at the headteacher. 'I'm still convinced that some of your pupils know more than they're letting on.'

The headteacher looked worried again and Alistair Marshall allowed himself a slight smile; at least someone else was having a crap day. Once everyone was out in the corridor, the detectives were approached by Angie Coulson.

'Any word on Lee?' she asked.

Marshall shook his head.

'He's got a lot of questions to answer, hasn't he?' said the teacher. She sighed. 'The head is right; this is very difficult for our pupils. And for the staff.'

'Sorry,' said Marshall. 'But until we know what's been happening, there's nothing we can do.'

Angie nodded.

'You'll do your best,' she said and walked off along the corridor. 'I know that, Alistair.'

Butterfield watched her go.

'I reckon she's got a thing for you,' she said.

* * *

A uniformed officer led Rad into the interview room at the Newcastle police station where he was being held. Garside and Harris were waiting for him, sitting grim-faced behind the desk. The other person in the room was a thin man in a suit, the duty solicitor, who was reading through his notes. Rad eyed them calmly; he did not seem perturbed by the situation in which he found himself.

'Take a seat, Rad,' said Garside. 'I think you already know DCI Harris from Levton Bridge Police Station. He wants to ask you a few questions as well.'

'I had nothing to do with the deaths of them girls, if that's what you are thinking,' said Rad. He sat down. 'You're not pinning murder on to me, so you can stuff your questions.'

'But we know that you have been trafficking drugs all across the north, including what looks like MDMA,' said Garside. 'The girls in Levton Bridge died after taking

MDMA and we think that your organisation is responsible for selling it to them.'

'Think what you like.' Rad glanced at the solicitor. 'They've got nothing to link me with them girls and I'm not making any comment.'

'It's your right,' said the lawyer.

'To be honest, Mr Letts, we don't need your client to comment,' said Garside. 'We've already got enough evidence to send you away for a long time. The knife next to your bed and the amount of drugs in the house is enough on its own. Care to explain that, Rad?'

'No comment.'

Harris leaned forwards.

'Come on, son,' he said. 'Do yourself a favour. Tell me about Lee Smedley.'

'I hardly know him.'

'But he was in your house.'

'So? He's a mate.'

'And how come he was there?' asked Harris.

'No comment.'

'We think he came to see you because he knows how much trouble he's in.'

'No comment.'

And with that Rad sat back in his chair, crossed his arms and stared defiantly at the detectives. An hour later, a frustrated Harris and Garside walked out into the corridor, where Matty Gallagher was waiting.

'How'd it go?' asked the sergeant.

'No comment,' said Harris.

* * *

Back in Levton Bridge, the uniformed sergeant unlocked the cell and walked in to see an unshaven Jason Craig sitting on the bench.

'You're free to go,' said the officer.

'About fucking time,' said Craig. He stood up. 'I'll be making a formal complaint about Jack Harris over the way I've been treated.'

'It's up to you, but I wouldn't recommend it.'

'Why not?'

'I just wouldn't. Anyway, I have a message from DCI Harris. He says that he is only releasing you under investigation and that he may be in touch again.'

'I want to see him.'

'He's not here,' said the officer.

'Where is he? Raiding that address I gave him in Newcastle?'

'I am not at liberty to divulge that information.' The sergeant led Craig out into the corridor. 'But before he went out, he asked me to tell you that you are to leave the town immediately.'

'Why should I? It's a free world, I can do what I like.'

'I'm just passing on the message. There's a bus for Newcastle that leaves from the top of the hill in twenty minutes. If I were you, I'd be on it.'

'This is a police state!'

'So I've been told,' said the sergeant in a bored voice.

Chapter twenty

'I'm not sure about this, Jack,' said Philip Curtis. He frowned at the inspector across the desk. 'Going public about Lee Smedley crosses a lot of lines.'

It was shortly after 2:00pm and he and Harris were sitting in the divisional commander's office at Levton Bridge Police Station, the inspector having just returned from Newcastle. It was time, Harris had decided, for drastic action, a feeling that he had to wrest back the initiative – a feeling that had grown on the journey back to Levton Bridge, Matty Gallagher sleeping most of the way, leaving his boss alone with his thoughts as he guided the Land Rover back towards his beloved northern hills.

Harris had suspected that the commander would need persuading about the wisdom of what he was suggesting and the uneasy expression on his face only served to strengthen the conviction.

'I know it's out of the ordinary,' said Harris. He took a sip of tea from his mug. 'But he's a suspect in a murder case and I have absolutely no idea where he is – and that scares the life out of me.'

'Yes, me too, but he's only fifteen.'

'And the age of criminal responsibility is ten.'

'I appreciate that, Jack, but naming Smedley in an appeal? Splashing his picture all over the media? Isn't that going a bit far? I mean, technically, he is still a child.'

'And a potentially dangerous one,' said Harris. 'We'd name him if he was an adult, wouldn't we? Indeed, things have only got as bad as they are with him because too many people have been treating him as a child. Lee Smedley should be viewed as someone who is capable of any crime that an adult may commit. That was the point I was trying to make at the council meeting yesterday.'

'I appreciate that, Jack, and I can see the validity of the argument. I'm just not sure everyone else will. I'll have to get special dispensation from the chief, for a start. God knows what he'll say. He's already on edge after the protests yesterday. Is there nothing else we can do?'

'Like what? We can't launch a search for him because we have no idea where to start. He could be anywhere. He could still be in Newcastle or he could be heading down to Blackpool. Or he could also be going somewhere else, for all we know. He's a free spirit is Lee Smedley and before he was sent to Rowan House he had a record of absconding. Even turned up once in Glasgow.'

'And are you sure he's the one we want for the death of Annabelle Roper?' asked Curtis. 'I mean, really sure?'

'No.'

'You're still not?' Curtis raised an eyebrow.

'Not one hundred percent, no.'

'You're asking the force to take a big gamble on someone who may not be the one we're after. I hope you know what you're doing.'

'He's the best prospect we have. We know that he was with Annabelle the night she died, we know that he deals in drugs and we know that he's linked to one of the biggest drug trafficking gangs in the north.' Harris counted the points off on his fingers as he spoke. 'I'd say that it all makes for a pretty strong case.'

'Granted,' said Curtis. 'But he denies being responsible for what happened to Annabelle, doesn't he?'

'Trouble is, the lad's a born liar. When we lifted him for that burglary in Letcombe Street last year, he denied even knowing where Letcombe Street was until we told him that the shop-owners had CCTV showing him forcing the till open. I admit that he had me doubting myself for a few moments in that garden earlier today but Matty's right, Lee Smedley is totally untrustworthy and until we get to question him, we'll not bring this thing to a close.'

'I suppose so,' said Curtis. He glanced down at the photograph that Harris had brought into the office. Taken when Smedley was arrested for possession of cannabis, it showed the young man staring back at the camera, eyes glinting, a crooked smile playing on his lips, a smile that suggested that he knew more than he was letting on. 'But I do keep coming back to his age, Jack. Like it or not, he's only a teenager and, as such, he is entitled to some protections, anonymity for starters.'

'And your concern does you credit.'

Curtis searched the inspector's face for evidence that the comment was meant to be sardonic but found nothing; love him or loathe him, thought the commander, you were guaranteed honesty from Jack Harris. Curtis, well used to the politics involved in his role, had always appreciated that, even when he found himself in dispute with the inspector.

'However,' said Harris, sensing that the commander's resolve was wavering, 'we have issued appeals naming teenagers before. Eastern Division issued one for that lad they wanted after the stabbing at Abbey Farm. In fact, that's how they caught up with him.'

'But he was seventeen,' pointed out Curtis. 'Smedley's fifteen. The media wouldn't be allowed to name him in a court case, would they? What you are suggesting, is exceptional. The civil liberties people will be jumping up and down if we go through with it.'

'If you want to talk about exceptional, then just think about what's happened over the past month. A town in uproar and two kids dead.'

Harris let the commander digest the comment. As the silence lengthened. The inspector thought back to the worried parents who had approached him following the protest outside Rowan House the previous day. Thought back to Annabelle Roper sprawled in the copse, her body defiled by vicious scratches, to David Roper's fury mixed with tears of anguish, to his wife's crushing grief, to her hands twisting and untwisting the sodden handkerchief. To Maureen Cross's accusing stare when she asked him how Annabelle's death had been 'allowed to happen'. And the inspector thought – and it was the first time he had found his mind straying back to Kosovo for many hours – of the bodies of the dead children lying in the forest clearing, staring up at leaden skies through lifeless eyes.

'I know what I am asking is out of the ordinary, sir,' he said eventually. There was an urgency to his voice. 'But we have to do something. What's the other option? Sitting on our hands? I don't think so. People in this town are looking to us to keep their children safe. They already think we've not done enough.'

'I appreciate that but–'

'How would we feel if it turns out that we are right and Smedley *is* the one who supplied the MDMA? If another girl dies and we could have done something to prevent it but didn't because we pussyfooted around the thought that he was still a child? We have a duty to warn people.'

'Yes, but surely every kid in this town already knows about him?'

'But what about other towns, other villages, other kids?' Jack Harris shook his head. 'I, for one, am not prepared to take that risk. It's not that long since your daughter was fifteen – how would *you* feel?'

Philip Curtis went on his own journey through the shadows of Memory Lane. Thought back to when his daughter was the same age as Annabelle Roper, recalled the dismissive way she reacted to his lectures on drugs, relived vividly again the worry that he experienced when she was back later than expected in the evening, felt once again the way that he had always jumped when the phone rang and the relief he felt when he heard the front door open and knew that she was safe – at least for one night. He picked up his desk phone and punched in a number.

'Jane?' he said. 'Can you get me the chief, please? Yes, it's urgent.'

'Thank you,' said Harris.

Five minutes later, the inspector was on his way to the office, planning to take the dogs out for a short walk in the nearby park, when Gallagher approached along the corridor.

'How did it go with Curtis?' he asked.

'He's checking with the chief. Are you looking for me? Because if it's bad news, I don't want to know.'

'Not sure what it is,' said Gallagher. The officers started walking down the corridor. 'It's about Jason Craig.'

'What about him?'

'Well, when the custody sergeant released him this morning, he delivered your message about getting out of town.'

'And?'

'And he didn't. Alison spotted him having a cup of coffee in Blueberries a quarter of an hour ago. Do you want us to pick him up?'

'For what? It's not against the law to have a cup of tea. Some of Heather's cakes are criminal, mind.'

'Well done,' said Gallagher. 'My campaign on developing your sense of humour is coming on nicely.'

Harris scowled at him but the sergeant knew that he didn't mean it.

'So we leave him be?' asked Gallagher.

'Unless he starts agitating again. Have you checked if he has been back on Facebook?'

'He hasn't. In fact, your warning seems to have done the trick. They're all keeping pretty quiet. The odd comment but nothing on the scale we were seeing before. Even Miriam Canley has been keeping herself to herself.'

'Good. We've got bigger problems to worry about.'

'Well, hopefully this isn't one of them. It came into the squad room a few minutes ago.' Gallagher handed Harris a scrap of paper on which was scrawled the name Jeremy Callard and a telephone number. 'That's an international number, isn't it?'

'It is.' Harris glanced at it thoughtfully. 'It is indeed.'

'You think Smedley may be trying to get out of the country?'

'No, it's nothing to do with what's happening here.'

Gallagher looked at him intently.

'Anything I need to know about?' he asked.

'Not really.'

And with that, Harris turned into his office and closed the door. Matty Gallagher stood outside for a few moments, deep in thought. Not that he would ever tell the inspector that he had done it, but he had Googled the phone number and knew that the call came from the International Criminal Court.

In the office, Harris sat down at his desk and produced some treats from a drawer and tossed them to the expectant dogs.

'We'll have a walk round the park in a few minutes,' said the inspector. 'Just got to sort something out first.'

He fished his mobile phone out of his jacket pocket, sat and stared at the piece of paper for a few moments then rang the number.

'Jeremy Callard,' said a cultured voice.

'It's Jack Harris.'

'Ah, Jack, thanks for ringing back. Have you had a chance to think about what we talked about?'

'I have, yes,' said Harris. 'To be honest, I've thought of little else.'

'And?'

'And yes, I'll provide whatever information you need. Like I said before, though, we arrived in the clearing the best part of a day after the massacre had taken place so I'm not sure how much use my testimony will be.'

'I appreciate that,' said Callard. 'But, like I told you before, our Kosovan informants have given us enough to link the killings to the perpetrators, what you can provide is an eyewitness account of the aftermath. You can do that, can't you?'

Harris's mind went back to the bodies in the clearing again. To the dead children. To the acrid taste of bile rising in his throat. To the shock on the faces of the other soldiers.

'I am afraid I can,' he said. 'I'd managed to put the image to the back of my mind for years but this has brought back so many memories.'

'There's always a danger that that can happen. Did you think more about my suggestion about counselling? You didn't receive any at the time, as I recall.'

'The Army did offer it,' said Harris. 'Some of the lads took them up on the offer but I didn't.'

'The Army is changing, Jack. More aware that macho thinking does you no good, in the end. I really would recommend that you reconsider. I can put you in touch with someone if you want.'

'I'll think about it.'

'I'll text you her number anyway. I'll also be in touch about how we record your testimony. We'll probably send a couple of people over.'

'Give it a couple of days, will you?' said Harris. 'I've got some other things to deal with first.'

'Yes, I saw it on Sky. A couple of dead teenagers, I think? Might I suggest that that is all the more reason to take up the offer of counselling? A case like that can stir up all kinds of strong emotions and with us dredging up all this stuff about what happened in Kosovo as well; well, I'm just saying… don't let it eat you up. I'll be in touch.'

And with that the line went dead.

Chapter twenty-one

'You want to do what?' asked James Hall, staring across the desk at Harris in amazement.

'We are going to issue a media appeal for information on the whereabouts of Lee Smedley,' said the inspector. 'We will say that we want to talk to him in connection with the death of Annabelle Roper.'

'You're crazy!'

It was just after 5:30pm and the two men were sitting in the manager's office at Rowan House. The atmosphere crackled with tension as Hall stared at the detective through narrowed and suspicious eyes. Harris remained calm but prepared to fight his corner. Both men knew that it was the confrontation that was always going to come between people on different sides of a massive divide.

'But he's only a child,' said Hall. The anger had dissipated and the voice sounded smaller. 'Are you even allowed to do that?'

'We have obtained permission, yes.'

'But think of the damage this could cause to him.' Hall shook his head. 'People like you just don't understand. All I have ever wanted to do is look after these children. Set them straight, give them a chance of a decent life and—'

'I appreciate your concern for the boys under your care.'

'Like that's true.' Hall snorted.

'Actually, it is.'

Harris found himself surprised by the words coming out of his mouth but something about the crushed demeanour of the man had touched a nerve and recent events had already led him to do a lot of thinking. He had been forced to challenge a lot of the convictions that he had long held.

'I know that Lee Smedley is, in many ways, still a child and that you have a responsibility to care for him,' said Harris. His tone was softer, more conciliatory, realising that the manager was also witnessing the crumbling edifice of much of what he believed in. 'I admire that, I really do, but I can't ignore what has been happening in this town. Surely, you realise that.'

'I suppose so. It's just so difficult to take.'

'I know but the truth, hard as it may be to accept, is that, in many ways, Lee Smedley is also an adult capable of adult actions. I'm sorry, James, but everything points to him having an involvement in Annabelle Roper's death. I can't turn a blind eye to that.'

'And can you be sure?'

'He's certainly got some questions to answer. Like why he fled town, for starters.'

'He often does it after a burglary. Keep out of the police's way.'

Harris gave him a look.

'You can see why we don't trust you, can't you?' he said.

'I suppose so,' said Hall ruefully. 'Anyway, it's true. Then I imagine he panicked when he saw that Annabelle was dead.'

'I'd like to hear that from his own mouth.'

'Well, I still don't like the idea of a media appeal, Chief Inspector. I don't like it all. What do Annabelle's parents think?'

'My detective inspector is with them now.'

* * *

'You want to do what?' said David Roper. He stared at Gillian Roberts, aghast at what he was hearing.

'We wish to issue a media appeal for information on the whereabouts of Lee Smedley in connection with the death of your daughter,' said the detective inspector.

'Well, I'm not sure about this.'

Roberts and DC Alison Butterfield were sitting in the Ropers' living room. Glenis was twisting and untwisting her handkerchief again.

'Don't you want us to track down the person we think is responsible for your daughter's death?' asked Roberts.

'Yes, of course I do. It's just...' David Roper sighed. 'I suppose it's the idea of people thinking about our lovely daughter being assaulted by that awful boy. It's a horrible image to carry around with you.'

'I get that,' said Roberts. 'But if he is responsible, we need to get to him before he does the same thing to anyone else. Another Annabelle.'

Glenis Roper gave a sob but said nothing.

'I take it you think this is the only way?' asked her husband.

'We do, yes. We have been told that Lee Smedley and another boy from Rowan House were with Annabelle the night she died.'

'What other boy?' asked Roper.

'I'm not at liberty to—'

'Was it Danny Cairns?'

'What makes you say that?' asked the detective inspector.

'I'm a governor at Roxham Comp. You get to hear things from the staff. One of the teachers told me that the two of them are thick as thieves.'

'Which teacher?'

'Angie Coulson,' said Roper. 'She is Danny Cairns' form tutor. I take it you have talked to Danny?'

'We have. He says that your daughter was alive when they left her and we've got nothing to say otherwise. However, a lot of things are pointing at Lee Smedley.'

'And there's no other way apart from this appeal?'

'We'd probably get him eventually but DCI Harris is of the opinion that we need to move quickly. We need to find out how much more of this MDMA is in circulation. We got close to Smedley in Newcastle this morning but he managed to escape.'

'Those raids on the television?' asked Roper. 'The County Lines? Is that what this is all about?'

'We think so.'

'And do you need our approval to issue this media appeal?'

'Approval, no, but your blessing would help.'

Roper looked at his wife, who had continued to sob.

'Do what you have to,' he said. 'There's one thing, though. I don't want my daughter's picture splashed all over the media next to one of that animal.'

'We can ask the journalists to be responsible about it,' said Roberts. 'But I can't promise anything. You know what they're like.'

* * *

'This will destroy Rowan House,' said Hall. He slumped in his chair and closed his eyes. It seemed to Harris that he was close to tears.

'Lee Smedley is only one boy,' said the inspector. 'Surely people will not judge you on a single case?'

'You did. You stood up in that council meeting and wrote off Rowan House based on what he was doing. Him and Danny Cairns. We have fifteen boys here and most of them are doing really well.'

'Point taken.'

'It's probably too late anyway,' said Hall with a sigh. 'Everything that we have tried to do here is ruined. I've already had the organiser of the awards on saying that they are thinking of withdrawing our nomination.'

'You know my views on awards,' said Harris. 'But I realise that this is hard for you. I know that you've dedicated yourself to this.'

Hall gave him a grateful look.

'Thank you,' he said. 'At least someone gets it. All those people protesting outside this place yesterday don't. Jason Craig doesn't. And I've just come off the phone with Gerald Gault, who wants to see me on Friday. Apparently, he's coming under "extreme political pressure".'

'Straw men,' said Harris.

'Straw men with the power to destroy everything I have worked for, Chief Inspector. I take it that you don't need my approval to make this appeal? You're going to do it anyway?'

'I am afraid so but as his legal guardians you need to know. The appeal will be issued to the media within the hour.'

'Can I ask one favour? I very much doubt that the media will handle the story sensitively – can you bring some pressure to bear?'

'We can ask,' said Harris. 'But we have no influence over the way the story is reported.'

'Then don't issue the appeal.'

'Too late for that,' said Harris.

Chapter twenty-two

'So much for asking them to be sensitive,' said Harris.

It was shortly after 8:00pm and he was standing in the CID squad room, part of a gathering of officers who clustered round Matty Gallagher's desk to stare grim-faced at the image that the sergeant had just called up on his computer. It was the online version of the next morning's front page of one of the national tabloids. The headline, presented in large bold type above pictures of Annabelle Roper and Lee Smedley, was *Beauty and the Beast*.

Harris glanced at Gillian Roberts, who was standing next to him.

'Not exactly what I had in mind,' he said.

'What did you expect?' said Roberts. 'You know what journalists are like. One thing's for sure, David Roper will not be impressed.'

'Nor James Hall,' said Harris. 'It's just a question of which one rings up first.'

The desk phone rang. Harris grimaced.

'I didn't even have time to set up a sweepstake,' said Gallagher. 'Care to guess who it is?'

No one replied and he lifted the receiver to his ear, listened for a moment then handed it to Harris.

'David Roper,' he said.

'You call that fucking responsible!' exclaimed Roper furiously when Harris answered. 'Have you seen what they've done with my daughter's picture? I told you I didn't want the two of them next to each other.'

'I apprecia–'

'I've had to call the doctor to Glenis. She collapsed when she saw that front page. You've not heard the last of this, Harris. I'll have your career.'

He slammed down the receiver and, before Harris could say anything, the desk phone rang again. Harris picked it up this time.

'It's James Hall,' said a voice. 'I hope you're proud of yourself.'

'I told you–'

'I've just had Gerald Gault on the phone about Friday's meeting. They want to close us down. I told you the media would not be sensitive about it. Thank you very much, Chief Inspector.

The line went dead. Harris looked round at the other detectives.

'Off the Christmas card list?' said Gallagher brightly.

A number of the detectives smiled but Jack Harris was not one of them.

'I just hope we made the right call,' he said.

Before anyone could reply, the desk phone rang again.

'More fans,' said Harris gloomily.

Gallagher picked up the receiver, listened for a few moments, jotted something down and replaced the phone.

'We made the right call, alright,' he said. 'That was one of the guys who drives the bus that comes over from Newcastle. He's just seen the front page and reckons he brought Lee Smedley over this afternoon.'

Harris perked up.

'Excellent,' said the inspector. 'He's back in Levton Bridge then?'

'Probably not. The driver says Smedley asked him to stop the bus after it left Roxham. Just where the moorland begins.' Gallagher looked down at the piece of paper. 'Nawton. That's that little place with only one row of houses, isn't it?'

'That's it,' said Harris. 'Did Smedley say why he wanted to get off there?'

'Told the driver he was going hiking. The guy said he had a haversack with him. Reckoned it looked new. Didn't James Hall say that Smedley is into survival skills? Bear Grylls, that sort of thing?'

'He did,' said Harris.

'What do you want to do?' asked Gillian Roberts. 'It's too dark to look for him now, surely?'

'Yes, it is.'

Harris walked over to the large map on the wall and traced his finger to Nawton then across the large expanse of moorland.

'Big area,' said Roberts.

'Yeah, and just about nobody lives there,' said Harris. 'The next village is a good ten miles away. If he knows what he's doing, he could hide out there for days.'

'So what's the plan?' asked the detective inspector.

Harris turned away from the map.

'Can you liaise with uniform?' he said. 'Get as many bodies as we can for first light? Oh, and see if the chopper is available, will you? I'll ring Bob Crowther at mountain search and rescue, see if they can help us. No one knows the hills better than them. The rest of you, get onto anyone you know in the area and get the word out. Alison, you know the farmers, see if they've seen him.'

'Guv.'

The room was all activity as officers grabbed for their phones. In the middle of the hubbub, the DCI's mobile phone rang. It was Doc.

'Hawk,' said the pathologist. 'Sorry to trouble you at this time of night, although it sounds like you're still working.'

'I am afraid so. What can I do you for?'

'Those DNA samples you took from Danny Cairns and Tracey Malham. Just to let you know that they don't match the DNA taken from the scratches on Annabelle Roper's body.'

'As one door opens, another one closes, eh?'

'Sorry, old pal.'

Harris ended the call and walked over to the desk where Alistair Marshall was scrolling through his mobile phone contacts list for the friend with whom he had occasionally gone mountain biking across the moor.

'Alistair,' said Harris. 'Doc has been back on – Cairns and Malham are in the clear over Annabelle Roper.'

'That just leaves us with Lee Smedley then?'

'In theory,' said Harris.

'You still not sure?'

'Not entirely, Alistair. I still can't help feeling that we're missing something.'

As Harris walked back across the office, Marshall's mobile rang. The constable took the call.

'DC Marshall,' he said. 'Who is this, please?'

'It's Angie. From the school. You sound busy.'

'Just a bit. What can I do you for?'

'Well, I was going to take you up on that drink you mentioned but if you're busy...'

Marshall looked round at the bustle of activity in the squad room.

'It's not a good time really,' he said.

'Has something happened?'

'Lee Smedley has been spotted on the moors. Near Nawton.'

'I saw the appeal you put out. You still think it's him then?'

'It's looking that way,' said Marshall. 'You in at work tomorrow?'

'Yes. Why?'

'I am thinking that it may be worth talking to Danny Cairns again. We now know that he had nothing to do with Annabelle's death. Maybe that will allay his fears about the police and persuade him to give us more information about Lee.'

'How do you know that he wasn't involved?' asked Angie. 'Have you come up with something new?'

Marshall looked across the room to where Harris was running a finger across the map. He heard again the DCI's voice from the constable's first day in CID. *Don't tell them anything that you don't want anyone else to know.*

'I'm sorry, Angie,' said the constable. 'But I can't really go into that.'

'You can trust me. I won't tell anyone.'

'Really I can't. Look, I'd love to see you for a drink but now really is not the time. Talk tomorrow?'

'Sure.'

Marshall ended the call and stared at the phone for a few moments. Just for a second, a fleeting second, she had sounded frightened. He'd heard that tone in her voice before, back in the classroom when she had apologised for being sharp with him. However, it had only lasted a second and Marshall had decided that he had imagined it anyway. He stood up and walked over to Harris.

'Guv,' he said. 'Can I have a word?'

Chapter twenty-three

James Hall concluded his angry telephone call to Jack Harris, slammed the phone down and cursed. He reached out to switch off his computer. He'd had enough of the day and it was time to go home. There came a knock on his office door.

'Come in,' said the manager.

Danny Cairns entered the room.

'Danny,' said Hall. 'To what do I owe the honour?'

The teenager slid his mobile phone across the desk and pointed to the item on screen, a Facebook link to the tabloid newspaper report on Lee Smedley.

'You seen this?' said the teenager. He sat down at the desk.

'I am afraid I have,' said Hall. 'I tried to stop them doing it but DCI Harris was having none of it. He seems convinced that Lee killed Annabelle Roper.'

'Well, he's wrong.' Cairns took back his phone and slipped it into his trouser pocket. 'Lee wouldn't do something like that.'

'What makes you say that?'

'I just know.'

'How do you know? Is there something you want to tell me?'

'Just that Lee didn't do it,' repeated Cairns. 'He'd never do that. He liked Annabelle. And he had nothing to do with what happened to Ellie either.'

'Convince me.'

'He never dealt in MDMA, for a start. Just weed.'

'The police seem to think that he sells other drugs.'

'The police have got it in for Lee,' said Cairns. 'And it ain't right.'

'But you have to admit that it does not look good, Danny. I mean, you yourself have admitted that the two of you were with Annabelle the night she died and Lee did flee the town immediately afterwards, did he not? That's not exactly the actions of an innocent man.'

'He was frightened,' said Cairns.

'I don't think Lee does frightened.'

'Well. He was.'

'You've heard from him, I take it?'

'Maybe,' said Cairns.

'So why did he run?'

'He knew how it looked. He knew that the police would be looking for him after the burglary, then he heard that Annabelle was dead. He was scared that the police would pin it on him. Everyone knows that Jack Harris would fit him up, for sure.'

'DCI Harris has a lot of flaws, Danny, but I do not think he is the type of person who would fabricate the evidence. As for Lee, he's the one who ran away, isn't he?'

'Like I said, he was scared.'

'*You* weren't scared, Danny. You didn't run away. That's why they think it's Lee and not you.'

'Well, I'm just saying that Lee didn't do it,' said Cairns. He stood up and headed for the door. 'You tell Jack Harris that.'

'Do you know who did supply the drugs?' asked Hall.

Cairns turned back to face the centre manager. Hall sensed a change in his demeanour. Suddenly, the teenager was more wary.

'Na,' he said eventually.

'I don't believe you.' Hall leaned forward. 'Listen, Danny, if you know who gave those girls MDMA, now is the time to tell me. For Lee's sake, if nothing else. You have to tell the police what you know.'

'I ain't telling them nuttin'. I'll never do that.'

'Then I'm not sure you are doing much to help Lee. They'll catch up with him sometime. Bound to. The television report said that some of the police officers who raided those houses in Newcastle this morning were armed. If Lee isn't careful, he'll get himself shot.'

Cairns looked alarmed.

'They wouldn't do that!' he exclaimed.

'Why give them the chance? Look, if you don't want to tell the police then tell me instead, and I'll tell them.'

Cairns considered the comment.

'I daren't,' he said eventually.

'Why not?'

'Because I could get myself in trouble. You've seen what happened to Annabelle.'

'What does that mean? *Were you* there when she died? Should the police be talking to you instead of Lee? Did you come to see me because you want to tell me what really happened?'

'I came here to help Lee, that's all.'

'Then it's time to talk.'

Cairns headed for the door again.

'I'll think about it,' he said. 'I may tell you in the morning.'

'Promise?'

'I ain't making no promises.'

Hall sat back in his chair; he realised that there was little point in pushing it.

'OK,' he said. 'Come and see me before you go to school if you want to talk again. In the meantime, go and see if Freddy's had any thoughts about supper. He's in the office, I think.'

Cairns nodded and gratefully left the room. James Hall sat in silent thought for few moments then glanced across at the window as a movement caught his eye. The curtains had not been drawn and he thought for a moment that he had seen a shape in the deepening shadows. Fearing a return of the protestors, the manager walked quickly over and peered out but, to his relief, saw nothing. The path running along the side of the house was clear.

'Must be going mad,' he murmured.

Stifling a yawn and suddenly feeling immensely weary, he reached his jacket down from the peg on the wall, slipped it on, pocketed his keys and headed for the door where he snapped out the light. Having locked the door, he made his way along the corridor, nodding to a couple of the boys on the way. Just before he reached the front door, Hall popped into the office where a bearded young man was catching up on paperwork.

'All quiet, Freddy?' said Hall.

'Yeah, thank God. I wondered if some of the protestors would come back but we haven't seen anyone for hours. It's all quiet on Facebook as well. Couple of comments but nothing heavy.'

'Hopefully, they got the message. I told Danny that you might fix him some supper.'

The bearded man glanced at the wall clock. It read 8:45pm.

'Yeah, it's that time, isn't it?' he said and stood up. 'Any word on Lee?'

'Still missing, as far as I know,' said Hall.

'You see that report on the newspaper website?'

'I am afraid so. Danny saw it, too. Came to tell me that Lee has got nothing to do with those girls.'

'And do you believe him?' asked Freddy. He headed for the door.

'I don't know what I believe any more,' said James Hall. 'Listen, keep it under your hat, will you, but I think the council may be having second thoughts about keeping us open. I've been asked to see Gerald Gault on Friday.'

'We'll be alright. The council have got too much invested in this place.'

'I think not,' said Hall. 'Gerald Gault is panicking. So are the other councillors. Anyway, that's for Friday, I'm off home. You know where I am if you need me.'

A couple of minutes later, Hall was in the car park where he had just unlocked his vehicle when the sound of footsteps behind him attracted his attention. He turned and peered into the darkness but saw nothing at first. Then a familiar figure emerged from the gloom.

'What do you want?' asked Hall. 'I thought Jack Harris told you to get out of town.'

'I don't have to do what he says,' said Jason Craig. 'It's a free country.'

'What do you want anyway?' Hall tried to keep his voice steady, tried not to show the uneasiness he was feeling. He had never trusted Jason Craig and murder was in the air.

'I wanted you to know that this isn't over,' said Craig.

'What do you mean?'

'You'll see.'

And with that Jason Craig turned and vanished back into the shadows. An hour and a half later, Rowan House was silent and in darkness when one of the upstairs windows opened and a figure emerged and made its way down the drainpipe to the ground where it paused for a moment then headed in the direction of the road.

Chapter twenty-four

First light saw the police descend on Nawton village. Half a dozen vans parked up alongside the main Roxham road and disgorged their cargo of uniformed officers. Lights went on in house windows as the teams assembled and officers were dispatched to explain to the bemused residents what was happening in their normally quiet community. At the heart of the operation, Jack Harris strode among the officers, barking out commands, engaging in conversations with team leaders and making his point with a large map spread over one of the vehicle bonnets. Occasionally, he turned to waft a hand in the direction of the expanse of moorland which was coming into ever sharper focus as the morning light strengthened.

Out on the hills, the mountain rescue team were already a couple of miles away, picking their way steadily across the moor, their boots squelching on heather that was damp after a burst of overnight rain. They had been the first to arrive, their minibus pulling up several hundred metres outside the village when it still dark but with the first glimpses of dawn streaking the sky. Having parked up and assembled their equipment, the team leader had phoned Jack Harris, who had been a team member ever since he had arrived back in Levton Bridge to work. They had agreed the route that the team would take and the volunteers had set off.

The winds that had blown up overnight, bringing the rain with them, had died down but the moor was still blustery and the clouds had dispersed and ribbons of blue sky promised a pleasant day to come. The seven-strong team walked with steady and sure foot, a legacy of years spent traversing the northern hills together, and from time to time, one or other of them would stop to scan the hills through binoculars.

'Anything?' team leader Crowther would ask but the question was always greeted with shakes of the head.

After trekking for an hour, the rescue team heard the distant clatter of rotor blades and turned to watch as the force helicopter approached, sweeping low over the moorland as it made its first foray of what promised to be a long day. Crowther waved at the pilot as the aircraft passed overhead then he and his team resumed their steady progress. Half an hour later, they approached a place where the moors gave way to a gulley with trees ranged down its steep sides. Crowther stopped walking and thoughtfully surveyed the place through his glasses.

'Where would you spend the night if you wanted to avoid the wind?' he asked his deputy.

'Somewhere sheltered,' said Mike Ganton.

'Like that?' Crowther pointed to the trees.

'Like that.'

'That's what I thought.' Crowther fished his mobile phone out of his waterproof's pocket and dialled a number. 'Hawk? It's Bob.'

'Yes, Bob,' said Harris, who was still in Nawton. 'What you got?'

'There's a small patch of woodland. We reckon it's ideal for someone laying up overnight, especially with all the wind there was last night. Do you want us to check it out?'

'You'd better wait for me to send some officers,' he said. 'Lee Smedley may be dangerous.'

'That could take a while, though.'

'I know but–'

'Why not let us check it out? If we see your guy, we'll just back off. Even if he does try it on, there's seven of us against one of him. Your helicopter is circling around here so it can bring officers quickly enough if we need them.'

'I'm not sure, Bob. Our rules say that–'

'And when did you ever take any notice of rules, Hawk? Listen, if we have to go through this rigmarole every time we find somewhere that might be interesting, we'll never get anything done.'

Harris thought for a moment.

'Yeah, go on then,' he said. 'But be careful.'

The rescue team moved slowly as they dropped down into the gulley, holding onto straggling roots as they picked their way down the steep sides, eyes darting left and right for signs of movement. Further down, the gulley widened out and it was Mike Ganton who spotted the shelter first, pointing to the branches and the covering of leaves in the lee of a large rock. He crouched down nearby.

'What do you think?' he whispered to Crowther as the team leader joined him. 'Shall we call Hawk?'

'Let's check it out first. No point calling in until we know what the crack is. It looks deserted to me.'

Ganton nodded and the two men edged closer, hearts in mouths, pulses pounding. Crowther reached out and whipped away a couple of the branches to reveal evidence of recent occupation, a couple of chocolate wrappers and an empty baked bean tin. Exploring further, Mike Ganton discovered the remains of a fire a few metres away from the shelter. He reached down to run his finger through the ashes.

'Warm?' asked Crowther.

'Ish.' Ganton cast a nervous look around him.

Crowther fished his mobile phone out once more.

'Hawk, it's Bob again,' he said. 'Your guy was definitely here.'

'But he's not there now?'

'No, but he's not been gone that long.'

'Good work, Bob. Text me the grid reference, will you, and I'll get the chopper to drop a team over to you.'

'Do you want us to try to track him?' asked Crowther.

'No, stay there until my guys get there, will you? We'll need to secure the scene. Shouldn't be long.'

'But he might get away.'

'Even someone as fit as Lee Smedley can't get that far on foot. In fact...' Harris did not finish the sentence because he noticed Alison Butterfield waving frantically at him from the other end of the village. 'I'll get back to you, Bob, don't move and don't touch anything.'

'OK.'

Harris strode over to the approaching Butterfield, who was holding up her smartphone.

'That was the DI,' she said. 'She tried you on your mobile but you were engaged. The duty manager at Rowan House has just been on. Seems like Danny Cairns has gone AWOL.'

'Any idea when?'

'They're not sure. The manager saw him about elevenish and assumed he'd gone to bed but it has not been slept in and they only noticed that he was missing when he didn't turn up for breakfast.'

Harris dialled a number on his mobile phone.

'Gillian,' he said. 'What do we know?'

'Precious little,' said the detective inspector's voice. 'The duty manager reckons he got out of his bedroom window and climbed down a drainpipe. He's done it before.'

'Do they think he may be trying to link up with Smedley?'

'Nobody knows.'

'OK, do what you can. I'll come straight over. Have you got anyone to send up there in the meantime?'

'Yeah, Matty and Alistair are here.'

'Well, get them to go and have a chat with the staff. And ask them to see what James Hall has to say for himself.'

'Will do.'

Harris ended the call and walked over to the uniformed inspector.

'Gerry,' he said. 'I've got to get back to town but Bob Crowther has just been on. They've found some sort of a camp and—'

His phone pinged with the sound of a text arriving. Harris showed the inspector the co-ordinates.

'Do you think you can get the chopper to drop a couple of your lads there?' he asked.

'Yeah, sure.'

Harris was about to walk over to another of the uniformed officers when the mobile rang again. He looked down at the display and took the call. A sixth sense told him that it was bad news.

'Gillian,' he said. 'What you got?'

'Nothing you'll like,' she said. Her voice was flat. 'A woman walking her dog across the playing field off Kawby Road has found a body.'

Harris closed his eyes.

'Danny Cairns?' he asked.

'Sounds like it. It's certainly a teenager.'

'On my way,' said Harris. He watched the uniformed officers closing off the road so that the police helicopter could land, then let his gaze stray across the moorland to where a dark cloud had started to drift in over the tops. 'It never rains…'

Chapter twenty-five

'So, what do you think, Doc?' asked Jack Harris. 'We've been here before, haven't we?'

'I am afraid so,' said the pathologist. 'There's no way that this was accidental.'

Doc was crouched over the body of Danny Cairns, which was lying amid trees on the edge of a playing field on the fringes of Levton Bridge.

'You sure?' asked Harris.

'No doubt about it. It's supposed to look like what happened to Annabelle but it's not.'

'What makes you say that?'

Doc reached down and turned the teenager's head so that the inspector could see the caked blood matting the hair on the back of the scalp.

'That does,' he said. 'I reckon that, if a drug was administered, he was probably unconscious when it happened. He was given a pretty hefty whack.'

'Could it still have been accidental, though?' asked Harris. 'Maybe he took the drugs, became disorientated and fell and hit his head on something? A rock maybe?'

Doc glanced over the forensics officer who was searching a nearby area under the trees.

'You didn't find anything, did you?' he asked.

The forensics officer shook his head.

'Nothing,' he said. He wafted a hand in the direction of the playing field. 'We've yet to do a detailed search but we ran an eye over the whole area before we started and there's nothing obvious. Oh, and we still haven't found his mobile phone. We're assuming that he had one. I don't know a teenager who doesn't.'

'Sorry, Hawk,' said the pathologist, 'but you're looking at a re-run of what happened to Annabelle Roper.'

'So it would seem,' said the inspector grimly. 'Any idea when he died?'

'I'd say about midnight, one in the morning.'

Before Harris could reply, he spotted Matty Gallagher approaching across the field.

'Anything?' asked Harris.

'Maybe,' said the sergeant. He held up his notebook. 'One of the uniform lads was doing door-to-door at the new houses that run across the end of the field and he came across a guy who was walking his dog late last night and saw a car parked on the road, up by the main gate. A dark one. He thinks it might have been a Nissan Micra.'

'Did he get a reg?'

'Sorry,' said Gallagher. 'He did not really think anything of it. It was only our officer knocking on his door that made him think it might be important.'

'Do we know anyone with a dark Nissan Micra?'

'Only about a million people.'

'Anything else?' asked Harris.

'Well, when I rang James Hall to tell him about Danny, he asked to see us. Says he has something which may be of use.'

* * *

Twenty minutes later, the detectives were sitting in the manager's office at Rowan House. Hall's eyes were bloodshot and he had failed to conceal the tears that had rivered his cheeks.

'This is terrible,' he said in a voice that was quiet and broken. 'Poor Danny.'

'You said you had something to tell us,' said Harris.

'He came to see me last night. Just before nine o'clock.'

'What did he want?'

'To tell me that Lee had nothing to do with Annabelle Roper's death.'

'And did you believe him?' asked Gallagher.

'He seemed genuine, yes. I got the impression that he wanted to tell me something else. That he might have known who did kill her.'

'But he didn't tell you?'

'Said he would think about it. We agreed to talk again this morning. Or I did, anyway. I'm not sure he would have done so. I got the impression that he was frightened.'

'Frightened of what?'

'He said that we'd seen what happened to Annabelle.'

'Did he say anything else?' asked Gallagher.

'Danny didn't, no, but I also had a visit from Jason Craig last night. He waited for me in the car park.'

'And what did he want?' asked Harris, glancing at Gallagher, who looked as surprised as his boss.

'Wanted me to know that our dispute was not over.'

'And what did he mean by that?' asked Gallagher.

'I'm not sure. He said that I would see. Those were his exact words.'

Harris looked at his sergeant with narrowed eyes.

'I want Jason Craig arrested and I want it done now,' he said.

Gallagher nodded and left the room.

'We're finished,' said James Hall when the sergeant had gone. 'There's no way that the council will let us stay open after this. Do you think that Jason Craig killed Danny?'

'I am pretty sure he didn't,' said Harris.

'Lee then?'

'I'm suspecting that neither of them did.'

'But you've been going about claiming that Lee—'

'Well, we may have been wrong. We're pretty sure that Lee spent last night up on the moors over Nawton way. There's no way that he could have got back to kill Danny.'

'So who did?'

'The same person who killed Annabelle Roper,' said Harris. 'Probably the person who supplied the drugs to Ellie Cross as well.'

'Do you know who?'

'I've got my suspicions.'

'Care to tell me?'

'Not yet, but if we're right, your faith in Rowan House might be justified, after all. Danny Cairns is a victim, and from what you have just told us, one who may have been about to do the right thing by Annabelle Roper and Ellie Cross. No one can blame you for that.'

'You just watch them,' said Hall bitterly. 'The protestors'll have a field day on Facebook – and you know what councillors are like.'

Harris left the manager to his gloomy thoughts and walked out to the car park where Gallagher was standing by his vehicle, deep in conversation on his mobile phone.

'You sure?' said the sergeant. He listened for a few more seconds and ended the call. 'That was Alison, guv. Looks like Jason Craig may be out of the picture.'

'Why's that then?'

'One of his mates drove over from Newcastle to pick him up last night. As luck would have, he picked him up in the marketplace and the Co-op's CCTV picked him up getting into the vehicle.'

'Doesn't mean that he went home.'

'Except he did. One of Northumbria's speed cameras clocked the vehicle on the approach to Newcastle just before midnight. Doing eighty-one in a seventy zone. It's not the world's greatest picture but there were definitely two of them and the guy in the passenger seat looks like

Jason Craig. Northumbria are sending someone out to confirm it.'

'Which just leaves us with one suspect,' said Harris. He looked across as a vehicle entered the car park. 'Hopefully, here is someone who can tell us more.'

The car pulled to a halt and Alistair Marshall got out, clutching a brown A4 envelope.

'Well?' asked Harris.

Marshall slid a piece of paper out of the envelope.

'We were right to be suspicious,' he said.

'*You* were right to be suspicious,' said Harris.

'I wish I wasn't.' Marshall scanned the contents of the paper. 'Three convictions for supply when she was in her teens and living in Sheffield. Two for ecstasy. Probation for the first, a suspended sentence for the second. Oh, and an earlier one for trying to give cannabis to an eleven-year-old when she was fourteen. Two months in a juvenile centre for that one.'

'So how come she landed a job working with kids?' asked Gallagher. 'I thought schools were supposed to carry out background security checks.'

'They are but all the offences were in her maiden name.'

'I didn't know she was married,' said Harris.

'She's not but she claimed that she was on her job application. Said she was separated. The head was iffy about letting me see her application. I think he's terrified that their safeguarding procedures will be shown to be weak but I told him that the police were a bigger problem than Ofsted. Anyway, everything matches up. Date of birth, address etc.'

'Could still be a coincidence,' said Harris. 'Two and two makes five.'

'Don't think so. South Yorkshire Police rooted out a picture of her from her third arrest in Sheffield. It was a good ten years ago, and she's changed her appearance quite a bit but it's definitely her.'

'I don't suppose you know what kind of a car she drives, Alistair?'

Marshall nodded sadly.

'A Nissan Micra,' he said. 'I've seen her getting into it after school. A dark blue one.'

'Good enough for me,' said the inspector. He clapped his hands. 'OK, pick her up. Take Alison with you. And keep it low profile, will you? The last thing we want is something turning up on Facebook until we're sure.'

Marshall nodded and turned to go.

'Oh, Alistair,' said Harris.

The constable turned back.

'Guv?' he said.

'Good work. I know you had a thing for her.'

'I wish I was wrong,' said Marshall.

'So do I,' said Harris.

The inspector's phone rang. He glanced at the display and took the call.

'Gillian,' he said. 'What's happening?'

'They think they've located Lee Smedley. The search and rescue team spotted someone on the tops. Approaching High Hills Wood. They thought you might want to be there when they pick him up.'

Chapter twenty-six

Alistair Marshall walked along one of the corridors in Roxham Comprehensive, accompanied by the headteacher. The head stopped outside a classroom.

'This the one?' asked Marshall.

The headteacher nodded.

'I hope you're right,' he said.

'I hope I'm not,' said Marshall.

The headteacher pushed his way into the room where Angie Coulson was addressing the class, half-turned to point to the whiteboard on the wall. She started to smile as the headteacher entered the room, then saw Alistair Marshall standing behind him. The smile froze as she looked at the grim expression on the detective's face.

'Can I have a word, please, Miss Coulson?' said the headteacher.

Angie closed her eyes.

'Oh, God,' she breathed.

And in that moment, Alistair Marshall knew.

* * *

'Where did you last see him?' asked Harris as he scanned the hillside through his binoculars.

He and Bob Crowther were standing at the bottom of a hill, staring up at the steeply wooded slope which plunged down from the moor. It was difficult to see anything amid the closely packed evergreens and any noises were drowned out by the clatter of the helicopter's rotor blades as the aircraft hovered above them, its crew staring down and seeking movement.

'He was heading into the trees,' said the rescue team leader. 'Mike saw him.'

'And he's sure it was him?'

'Who else could it be? What's the plan? All that noise from the chopper is sure to have alerted him. Do you want us to—'

'The plan,' said Harris, 'is that you let us do our thing.'

The inspector glanced back towards the gathering of uniformed officers who had been dropped onto the moor in two trips from the force helicopter. A couple of them held guns. Crowther looked disappointed but nodded.

'Fair enough,' he said.

A few minutes later, the uniformed officers had fanned out and were heading up into the trees. Within a few moments, the woodland had swallowed them up and they picked their way carefully up slopes that were laced with shadows and slick from the overnight rainfall that had filtered through the boughs. Each officer shot wary glances left and right; they all knew that the fifteen-year-old was capable of being a savage opponent if cornered and all had been warned about his capacity for rapid movement.

It was Jack Harris who saw Lee Smedley first. The teenager was standing high above the detective on a rocky outcrop, staring down at them. For a few moments, their gazes met and Harris fancied that he could see a faint smile playing on the teenager's face.

'There's nowhere to run, Lee!' shouted Harris.

Smedley raised a hand then turned and started to sprint diagonally down the slope, careering wildly away from the police officers, recklessly hurdling fallen tree branches yet always landing safely without breaking his stride. Harris started to run, too, but cursed as he soon realised that he was no match for the swift-footed young man. It was then that another officer appeared in front of the teenager, having worked his way round the uppermost fringes of the wood unseen by his quarry. The teenager cried out in alarm as he saw him and veered back the way he had come but his path was blocked as more officers closed in.

Smedley dived towards where the trees petered out to allow the passage of a fast-flowing stream and started to slither at high speed down the slope, this time out of control, his feet slipping on the wet grass, his fingers grabbing frantically for a handhold as he gained momentum.

Seeing that Smedley's fall would take him close to his position, Jack Harris ducked behind a tree then stepped out. The teenager saw him too late. Harris grasped him by the shoulder, spinning him round and abruptly breaking his fall. Smedley squealed in pain and they struggled for a few moments as they rolled down the hillside, eventually coming to a stop beside the rushing waters of the stream where Smedley sprawled, clutching his injured shoulder, and where Harris's strength allowed him to gain the upper hand. Breathing hard, the inspector subdued the struggling teenager, forced him to his knees and handcuffed his hands behind his back.

One of the armed officers ran up to them and pointed the weapon at Smedley.

'Don't shoot!' cried the teenager, watching him with fear in his eyes. He looked at Harris. 'I didn't kill her.'

Harris hauled him to his feet.

'I know, son,' said Harris. 'I know.'

Chapter twenty-seven

Lee Smedley sat and stared across the table at Harris and Gallagher in the Levton Bridge Police Station interview room. Duty solicitor Mari Jameson sat next to the teenager.

'If you know I didn't kill Annabelle, why am I here?' asked Smedley. After his momentary loss of composure on the hills, he had regained his cocksure attitude. 'I reckon you have to let me go.'

'Well, that isn't going to happen,' said Harris. 'You're in more than enough trouble. They're going to throw the book at you, Lee, and this time there's no James Hall to bail you out. You'll not be going back to Rowan House, I can tell you that.'

'Why not?'

'Because the criminal justice system has had enough of you, sunshine.' Harris glanced down at a sheet of paper on the desk. 'Nine burglaries, including one on the night Annabelle was killed, numerous incidents of supplying cannabis to pupils at Roxham Comprehensive, acting as a courier for Rad and his band of merry men in Newc–'

'Yeah, but I never sold MDMA, just weed, so you can't fit me up with Annabelle's death.'

'We don't fit people up, Lee, and I'm sick of people saying that we do. Is that why you ran?'

'Yeah.'

'Well, like I said earlier, I am prepared to accept that you had nothing to do with what happened to Annabelle.'

'You are?'

'We are, yes.'

Smedley looked at him suspiciously but said nothing.

'So, where do we go from here?' asked the lawyer.

'It depends entirely on your client,' said Harris. 'Maybe it's time that he started acting like an adult.'

* * *

In the neighbouring interview room, Gillian Roberts and Alistair Marshall stared across the desk at Angie Coulson, who averted her eyes so as not to meet their gaze. A thin-faced man in a suit sat next to her; her lawyer.

'Why exactly is my client here?' asked the solicitor. 'You arrested her on suspicion of murder but I have heard nothing to support the allegation.'

'We believe that she forced Annabelle to take the doctored MDMA that killed her,' said Roberts. 'And we think that she killed Danny Cairns.'

'And where's your proof?'

'Perhaps your client would like to tell us where she was the night that Annabelle died?'

'I was at home,' said Coulson. It was the first time she had spoken since the interview had begun.

'Can anyone confirm that?' asked Roberts.

'No. I live alone.'

'Boyfriend?' asked Roberts.

Coulson shot Marshall a sly look.

'No,' she said. 'Mind, they don't know what they're missing.'

Marshall felt the bile rising in his throat and Roberts glanced at him to gauge his reaction. She and Harris had thought long and hard about letting the young detective take part in the interview because of his personal connection to the case. In the end, they had decided that the relationship that he had with Angie Coulson might prove useful.

Roberts glanced down at the print-out lying on the table.

'You have quite a record, Miss Coulson,' she said. 'Including supplying drugs to young people.'

'That's all behind me.'

'Are you sure?'

'Prove otherwise.'

Roberts reached for another piece of paper.

'We've checked your mobile phone,' said the detective inspector. 'Danny Cairns rang you last night.'

'So? They often ring me.'

'At midnight?'

'I was worried about him. A lot of the kids have been upset by what happened to Annabelle.'

'You do appreciate the seriousness of the situation, don't you?' asked the detective inspector. 'That withholding information is a crime?'

'You have to prove that I'm withholding it first,' said Coulson. 'And I don't think there's any way you can do that.'

A mocking smile flickered across her lips.

* * *

'Just tell me what you know,' said Harris, looking at Smedley wearily. The lack of sleep was catching up with him. 'I really am not in the mood for games.'

'What's in it for me?' asked the teenager. 'Will you let me off the charges if I do?'

Harris thought of the distressed victims of the houses that Smedley had burgled and shook his head.

'I can't promise that,' he said. 'Too many people around here think that you've been treated far too leniently as it is, me included. They won't stand for you being let off. You have to face the consequences of your actions some time, doesn't he, Sergeant?'

'Some time, yes.'

'However,' said Harris, 'I might be persuaded to put in a word on your behalf if you tell me what you and Danny were talking about on the phone last night.'

Smedley thought for a few moments then glanced at his lawyer.

'It's just about the best the police can do,' said the solicitor.

'Na,' said Smedley. 'Me and Danny have never been grasses. We've never spragged to the police and we ain't going to start now.'

'Danny's dead,' said Harris.

The inspector did not try to dress up the news in sympathetic language, did not try to cushion the blow. Time to play hardball. Smedley stared at him in disbelief. For the first time in all Harris's dealings with him, the teenager looked disturbed. Unsure. Shocked.

'Dead?' said Smedley eventually in a quiet voice.

'Yes, last night. Not long after you talked to him, oddly enough. We think he was murdered.'

'Murdered?' Smedley's voice was flat.

'Forced to take drugs, probably doctored MDMA like Annabelle. I think you know who did it.'

Smedley thought for a few moments then nodded.

'OK, OK,' he said. 'But I knew nothing about it until Danny told me last night. And he only found out the day Annabelle died.'

'Why didn't he tell us?'

'I told you, we don't sprag to the police. Besides, Miss Coulson told us that when it came down to it, nobody would take a scroat's word like his against that of a teacher. She reckoned you would think he was making it all up.'

'She was nearly right,' said Harris. He sat back in his chair, arms behind his head. 'From the beginning, please.'

* * *

As one hour stretched into two, Roberts and Marshall were growing increasingly frustrated by the stalling tactics of Angie Coulson. Question after question went unanswered and the detective inspector was beginning to worry that they might have to let her go. She was relieved when there came a knock on the door and Jack Harris strode into the room.

'Mind if I sit in?' he asked.

Roberts nodded and Angie Coulson watched him uneasily as he took a seat and placed a piece of paper on the desk.

'I've just been with Lee Smedley,' said Harris amiably. 'We had a nice chat, in fact. He's quite talkative when you get to know him.'

Coulson tried not to look worried.

'Would you like to know what he said?' asked Harris.

'It'll be nothing but a pack of lies,' said Coulson.

'I think not.' Harris's voice had an edge now. 'See, according to Lee Smedley, you've never quite shrugged off your old habit of giving drugs to young people. Lee reckons it's because you're a lonely person in need of company. He used somewhat more industrial language. He's quite prosaic when you get him talking but we'll let the shrinks work it out.'

Coulson said nothing.

'According to Lee,' continued the inspector, 'you recruited Ellie Cross and Annabelle Roper for your little evening soirees. They would come round to your flat, take some gear, enjoy a few drinks, listen to music. You knew they wouldn't tell their parents because of fear of getting into trouble. Besides, if there is one thing I have learned in the past month, it's that teenagers do like their secrets.'

Still, Coulson said nothing.

'However,' continued Harris, 'one night, you miscalculated. Plied Ellie with MDMA but her body could not cope. She got herself home and died in her bedroom.'

There was a flicker of emotion on the teacher's face.

'An accident,' said Harris. 'A genuine tragic accident but you knew that you'd probably get jailed for manslaughter and that your record meant it would be a long sentence. And when you came out, the career you had worked so hard to build would have been wrecked.'

Coulson remained silent.

'Your big problem,' said Harris, 'was that Annabelle was so horrified at what had happened that she threatened to tell her parents. You couldn't let her do that so you told her that no one would believe her and that, even if they did, her reputation would be ruined; that her dad would disown her, that the school would kick her out and that there was no way she would ever get into university.'

Coulson continued to say nothing. She did not need to; her eyes told their own story.

'Young Annabelle was made of stronger stuff, though,' continued Harris. 'After wrestling with it for a month, she told you that she could not keep her secret anymore. Told you that she planned to tell someone in authority, which is when you tricked her into going to the copse and forced her to take doctored MDMA. She fought for her life but in the end you were too strong.'

Coulson stared impassively ahead.

'Unfortunately for you,' said Harris, 'Annabelle had told Danny Cairns earlier that day. He'd always had a thing for Ellie and was appalled at what he was hearing about her death. He battled with his conscience – he's never been the type to tell the police anything, has Danny – but finally he decided to tell James Hall what he knew. So, you killed him as well. Lured him to the field, tricked him into taking the dodgy gear and whacked him.'

'Rubbish,' exclaimed Coulson, breaking her silence at last. 'All rubbish! Fairy tales. Lee Smedley has got it in for me.'

'I think not.' Harris turned fierce eyes on her and an image of the children lying in the forest clearing flashed into his mind. 'You're a predator, Miss Coulson, someone who preys on our young people when they are at their most vulnerable. You're scum.'

The teacher looked at him, startled by the venom in his voice. Roberts eyed him uneasily, wondering what would happen next. However, Harris did not add to his comment but sat back and eyed her with loathing.

'This is all lies,' said Coulson. She looked at her solicitor. 'Lies told by a good-for-nothing who just wants to get me in trouble because I don't let him mess about in class. I'm amazed that you believe it, Chief Inspector.'

Harris idly ran his fingers over the piece of paper lying on the table. Coulson watched him nervously. Finally, she could contain herself no longer.

'What's that?' she asked.

'This?' Harris glanced at the piece of paper as if he were seeing it for the first time. 'This is a comparison of your DNA and the DNA that was taken from scratch marks on the body of Annabelle Roper. And guess what? They only match.'

Angie Coulson was silent for a few moments then looked at the detectives through eyes that glistened with tears.

'I only wanted their company,' she said in a voice so soft that they could hardly hear it. 'I had no idea that the drugs would do that to Ellie. It just got out of hand. You have to believe me, Chief Inspector. I didn't mean for any of this to happen.'

'Maybe I *would* have believed you if you hadn't gone to the trouble of acquiring doctored drugs then covered up your actions. Personally, Miss Coulson, I think that you are as calculating as they come.'

'No, that's not—'

'You can cut the protestations.' His voice was harsh. Unforgiving. 'You knew exactly what you were doing giving Annabelle and Danny that drug. You betrayed the people who cared about you, Miss Coulson. The irony is that we probably would never have suspected you were it not for the actions of one of them, a rookie detective constable at that.'

The inspector looked at Roberts.

'Out of the mouths of babes, eh?' he said.

Chapter twenty-eight

Two days later, Jack Harris had just sat down at his desk and was waiting for the kettle to boil for the first cup of tea of the day when his mobile rang. It was Jenny. He smiled and took the call.

'Good morning,' she said. 'You got a minute?'

'Yeah. I'm not due at magistrates for Angie Coulson's remand until ten.'

'CPS sticking with two charges of murder and one of manslaughter?'

'They are. Coulson's going to play the mental health card when it comes to crown court, apparently, but the shrinks reckon she's fit to plead. Not my problem now.'

'You still think that someone supplied her with the doctored drugs?'

'Yeah. She won't tell us who but we're working with Sheffield. She still has contacts there. We'll get them.'

Harris sat back in his chair and put his feet up on the desk.

'Anyway,' he said, 'what can I do you for at this early hour?'

'I think I'm going to withdraw my name from the list for the Roxham job.'

'Why?'

'It's too early for us. I don't think you're ready and I sure as hell know I'm not. Besides, the M6 is not bad in the right light.'

'You sure about this?'

'Yeah. I think it's the right thing to do.'

'I'd have made it work, you know.'

'I know.'

'I have some news as well. I heard from Jeremy Callard again. He's sending a couple of people over the week after next. Asked if I mind meeting them in London. I wondered if you wanted to take a couple of days off and come with me? One of the girls is going to look after the dogs.'

'Doesn't sound like a particularly cheerful experience. Dead kids and all that.'

'I'll have plenty of spare time,' said Harris. 'It was Curtis who suggested it, actually. Said I needed a break.'

'He's right,' said Jenny. 'OK, I'll see what I can do, love. Given that Curtis knows, isn't it time you told Matty what's been going on?'

* * *

Ten minutes later, there came a knock on the door and Gallagher walked into the room.

'You wanted to see me?' he said.

'I do.' Harris gestured to a chair. 'Shut the door, will you?'

Gallagher did as he was requested and sat down.

'Am I in trouble?' he asked.

'Far from it. No, I think I owe you an explanation, Matty lad.'

'For what?'

'For why I have been acting so strangely.'

'Bloody hell, if you decided to do that, we'd be here all day! I do hope we're not in for a more fluffy Jack Harris.'

Harris smiled at the joke.

'No worries about that,' he said. 'No, you have asked me several times in recent days if something was wrong with me and I gave you all that stuff about kids and Jenny's job application.'

'Was it not true?'

'Only partly.' Harris hesitated, trying to marshal his thoughts. 'See, three weeks ago, I was approached by a man called Jeremy Callard. He's a lawyer who works for the International Criminal Court.'

'Ah, the call you received.'

'The very same.' Harris gave him a knowing smile. 'And if you were any kind of detective, you'd already know who he works for.'

'Who? Me?' Gallagher tried to look innocent. 'Why are you talking to them?'

'It dates from my time with the Army in Kosovo.' Harris's mind went back once more to the forest clearing. He felt strong emotions stirring and paused for a few moments to compose himself. 'I was one of a detail sent to investigate reports of a massacre. An entire village had been wiped out. There were kids among the dead.'

'And this Callard guy wants you to give evidence to some sort of hearing?'

'He does, yes. A couple of people have come forward naming the man who ordered the killings.'

'And are you going to do it?'

Harris nodded.

'It won't be easy,' said Gallagher. 'You talked to anyone about it?'

'Not for more than twenty years.'

'Then it's high time you did. I mean, a counsellor. Something like that can really fuck with your head.'

'Maybe.'

They talked for a few more minutes, then Harris glanced at the wall clock.

'I'd better go,' he said, standing up. 'Don't want to be late.'

* * *

The meeting in the office at County Hall had been under way for the best part of an hour and the four senior councillors, including Gerald Gault, had been listening to Jason Craig with increasing alarm. James Hall noted the councillors' worried expressions with a deepening despondency. There was no way that they would carry the day this time. Finally, Craig completed his testimony, sat back in his chair and looked triumphantly at James Hall.

'Well, thank you for coming over this morning, Mr Craig,' said the council leader. 'You have confirmed what we had already been thinking. The Rowan House experiment has been a failure. Do you have anything to say, Mr Hall?'

'What's the point?' said Hall, trying to control his anger. 'It sounds like you've already made up your mind.'

'I really cannot see much alternative,' said the leader. 'Mr Craig's account points to an appalling lack of discipline at Rowan House and we have to think of the council's reputation. I am sorry but—'

The door opened and Jack Harris walked in.

'Not too late, am I?' he said.

'This is a private meeting,' said the leader. 'Can I ask that you—'

'You can ask.' Harris sat down at the table and looked at Craig. 'I take it you've been regurgitating your usual poison, Jason?'

'I've told them the truth and—'

'Half the truth, I would suggest,' said Harris.

James Hall looked at him in surprise.

'You see,' said Harris, 'I've learnt a lot since I addressed the planning committee. Oh, don't get me wrong, gentlemen, I am still greatly concerned about the way Rowan House operates. Kids like Lee Smedley and Danny Cairns should not be allowed to go out and prey on this community but when it came down to it, both found it in themselves to stand up for what was right. Not, I would suggest, like the straw men in this room. You are far more interested in your reputations, might I suggest? What the voters will think of you.'

The councillors shifted uncomfortably in their seats.

'Yes, there need to be changes if Rowan House is to continue operating. Big changes.' Harris looked at James Hall. 'And maybe the people who work there have lost sight of their responsibility to the community, but they do care about the interests of the young men in their charge and that has to count for something.'

Jason Craig opened his mouth to speak but Harris beat him to it.

'May I suggest a way forward?' he said. 'That instead of fighting each other, we give Rowan House a second chance and work together to get it right? I may not agree with your tactics, Jason, but you have something to contribute, and my force is keen to work with the council as well.'

'But what about the protestors?' asked the leader. 'You speak big words about community but surely they have a right to be heard?'

'Then involve them.'

'They'll not like that.'

'Sometimes, gentlemen,' said Harris, 'you have to be brave.'

Ten minutes later, the battle won, the inspector walked into the corridor, thought of Miriam Canley and the protestors and smiled. That would teach them to assume that they knew which side he was on.

* * *

A week later, Jack Harris walked along the terraced city street and stopped in front of one of the houses. He checked the piece of paper in his hand against the brass plaque, hesitated then pressed the doorbell. Five minutes later, he was sitting in a tidy office looking at the woman in the armchair.

'So, tell me, Mr Harris,' she said. 'Why you have finally decided to seek counselling after all this time…?'

THE END

List of Characters

Miriam Canley – Levton Bridge parish council chairwoman and protestor
Jeremy Callard – international lawyer
Angie Coulson – teacher
Jason Craig – protestor
Andy Craig – Jason's brother
Ellie Cross – schoolgirl
Maureen Cross – Ellie's mother
Bob Crowther – Head of Levton Bridge Mountain Rescue Team
Doc – Home Office pathologist
Freddy – employee at Rowan House
Mike Ganton – Deputy Head of Levton Bridge Mountain Rescue Team
Gerald Gault – County Council planning committee chairman
James Hall – Rowan House manager
Mari Jameson – solicitor
Mr Letts – solicitor
Tracey Malham – schoolgirl
Martin Radcliffe (Rad) – drug dealer
Annabelle Roper – schoolgirl
David Roper – father of Annabelle Roper
Glenis Roper – mother of Annabelle Roper
Jane Rudge – mother of Lorna
Lorna Rudge – schoolgirl
Lee Smedley – teenage resident of Rowan House

If you enjoyed this book, please let others know by leaving a quick review on Amazon. Also, if you spot anything untoward in the paperback, get in touch. We strive for the best quality and appreciate reader feedback.

editor@thebookfolks.com

www.thebookfolks.com